Items should be returned on or before the last date shown below. Items not already requested by other borrowers may be renewed in person, in writing or by telephone. To renew, please quote the number on the barcode label. To renew online a PIN is required. This can be requested at your local library.
Renew online @ **www.dublincitypubliclibraries.ie**
Fines charged for overdue items will include postage incurred in recovery. Damage to or loss of items will be charged to the borrower.

Leabharlanna Poiblí Chathair Bhaile Átha Cliath
Dublin City Public Libraries

Dublin City
Baile Átha Cliath

Raheny Branch Tel: 8315521

Date Due	Date Due	Date Due
2 4 SEP 2012		

b.

TREADING ON DREAMS

Stories from Ireland

Irish writers have long been famous for short stories and there is a rich variety in this volume. On the windswept west coast of Ireland a boy and his grandmother welcome a stranger; in a Dublin bar two men discuss a woman. A mother struggles to live with the pain of a child's death; a failed musician drowns his sorrows in whiskey in New York. Then there is the fisherman who caught no fish; a small boy who gets cross with his father; and a girl with long black hair, cycling down the mountain road to her first party, with hope in her heart. And the wish in all their hearts might be, in the words of the poet W. B. Yeats, 'Tread softly because you tread on my dreams'.

BOOKWORMS WORLD STORIES

English has become an international language, and is used on every continent, in many varieties, for all kinds of purposes. *Bookworms World Stories* are the latest addition to the Oxford Bookworms Library. Their aim is to bring the best of the world's stories to the English language learner, and to celebrate the use of English for storytelling all around the world.

Jennifer Bassett
Series Editor

OXFORD BOOKWORMS LIBRARY

World Stories

Treading on Dreams

Stories from Ireland

Stage 5 (1800 headwords)

Series Editor: Jennifer Bassett
Founder Editor: Tricia Hedge
Activities Editors: Jennifer Bassett and Christine Lindop

He Wishes For The Cloths Of Heaven

Had I the heavens' embroidered cloths,
Enwrought with golden and silver light,
The blue and the dim and the dark cloths
Of night and light and the half-light,
I would spread the cloths under your feet:
But I, being poor, have only my dreams;
I have spread my dreams under your feet;
Tread softly because you tread on my dreams.

William Butler Yeats (1865 – 1939)

RETOLD BY CLARE WEST

Treading on Dreams

Stories from Ireland

OXFORD UNIVERSITY PRESS

OXFORD

UNIVERSITY PRESS

Great Clarendon Street, Oxford OX2 6DP

Oxford University Press is a department of the University of Oxford.
It furthers the University's objective of excellence in research, scholarship,
and education by publishing worldwide in

Oxford New York

Auckland Cape Town Dar es Salaam Hong Kong Karachi
Kuala Lumpur Madrid Melbourne Mexico City Nairobi
New Delhi Shanghai Taipei Toronto

With offices in

Argentina Austria Brazil Chile Czech Republic France Greece
Guatemala Hungary Italy Japan Poland Portugal Singapore
South Korea Switzerland Thailand Turkey Ukraine Vietnam

OXFORD and OXFORD ENGLISH are registered trade marks of
Oxford University Press in the UK and in certain other countries

ACKNOWLEDGEMENTS

The publishers are grateful to the following for permission to abridge and simplify copyright texts:
Lorcan Byrne for *Delivery* first published in *Phoenix Irish Short Stories 2003*; Brian Friel for
Mr Sing My Heart's Delight first published in *A Saucer of Larks*; Claire Keegan for *Men and Women* first
published in *Antarctica*; Edna O'Brien for *Irish Revel* first published in *The Love Object*; Peters Fraser
& Dunlop Ltd for *My Oedipus Complex* by Frank O'Connor first published in *Classic Irish Short Stories*;
Curtis Brown Group Ltd for *Poisson d'Avril (A Fishy Story)* by Somerville & Ross first published in
The Irish R. M.; Eamonn Sweeney for *Lord McDonald* first published in *Force 10* magazine; William
Trevor for *The Third Party* first published in *Good Housekeeping* magazine

Illustrated by: David Frankland

Word count (main text): 25,395 words

For more information on the Oxford Bookworms Library,
visit www.oup.com/elt/bookworms

CONTENTS

INTRODUCTION   i

NOTE ON THE LANGUAGE   viii

Mr Sing My Heart's Delight   1
Brian Friel

Irish Revel   12
Edna O'Brien

The Third Party   24
William Trevor

Delivery   37
Lorcan Byrne

My Oedipus Complex   47
Frank O'Connor

Men and Women   58
Claire Keegan

Lord McDonald   69
Eamonn Sweeney

A Fishy Story   79
Somerville & Ross

GLOSSARY   90

ACTIVITIES: Before Reading   93

ACTIVITIES: After Reading   95

ABOUT THE AUTHORS   99

ABOUT THE BOOKWORMS LIBRARY   101

NOTE ON THE LANGUAGE

There are many varieties of English spoken in the world, and the characters in these stories from Ireland sometimes use non-standard forms (for example, *ye* for *you*) or unusual patterns (for example, different word order in a sentence or a greater use of *will* and *would*). This is how the authors of the original stories represented the spoken language that their characters would actually use in real life.

There are also a few words that are usually only found in Irish English (for example, *eejit, Da, Mammy*). All these words are either explained in the stories or in the glossary on page 90.

Mr Sing My Heart's Delight

BRIAN FRIEL

❖

Retold by Clare West

On the west coast of Ireland there are wild, lonely places, where few visitors come. A boy on his yearly visit to his grandmother tells a tale of the simple life, when a travelling salesman from a faraway land finds a kindness he did not expect . . .

On the first day of every new year, I made the forty-five-mile journey by train, post van, and foot across County Donegal to my grandmother's house. It sat at the top of a cliff above the wild and stormy Atlantic, at the very end of a village called Mullaghduff. This yearly visit, lasting from January until the end of March, was made mostly for Granny's benefit; during these months Grandfather went across the water to Scotland to earn enough money to keep them going for the rest of the year. But it suited me very well too: I missed school for three months, I got away from strict parents and annoying brothers and sisters, and in Granny's house everything I did was right.

The house consisted of one room, in which Granny and Grandfather lived and slept. It was a large room lit by a small window and a door which could be left open for most of the day, because it faced east and the winds usually blew from the west. There were three chairs, a table, a bed in the corner, and an open fire, over which stretched a long shelf. All the interesting things in the house were on this shelf – a shining silver clock, two vases, a coloured photograph of a racehorse, two lifelike wooden dogs, and three sea-shells sitting on matchboxes covered with red paper. Every year I went to Granny's, these pieces were handed down to me, one by one, to be inspected, and my pleasure in them made them even more precious to Granny.

She herself was a small, round woman, who must once have been very pretty. She always wore black – a black turning grey with so much washing. But above the neck she was a surprise of strong colour: white hair, sea-blue eyes, and a quick, fresh face, browned by the sun. When something delighted her, she had a habit of shaking her head rapidly from side to side like a child, and although she was over sixty then, she behaved like a woman half her age. She used to challenge me to race her to the garden wall or dare me to go beyond her along the rocks into the sea.

Even on the best day in summer, Mullaghduff is a lonely, depressing place. The land is rocky and bare, and Granny's house was three miles from the nearest road. It was a strange place for a home. But Grandfather was a hard, silent man, who had married Granny when she was a girl of seventeen with a baby daughter (later to become my mother) but no husband. He probably felt he had shown enough kindness by offering to marry her, and the least she could do was accept the conditions of his offer. Or perhaps he was jealous of her prettiness and sense of fun, and thought that the wide ocean behind her and three miles of bare land in front of her would discourage any search for adventure. Whatever his reasons, he had cut her off so completely from the world that at the time of her death, soon after my thirteenth birthday, the longest journey she had ever made was to the town of Strabane, fifty-two miles away.

She and I had wonderful times together. We laughed with one

another and at one another. We used to sit up talking until near midnight, and then instead of going to bed, perhaps suddenly decide to eat fish fried in butter or the eggs that were supposed to be our breakfast the next day. Or we would sit round the fire and I would read stories to her from my school reading-book – she could neither read nor write. She used to listen eagerly to these, not missing a word, making me repeat anything she did not understand. After reading, she often used to retell the story to me ('Just to see did I understand right').

And then suddenly she would lose interest in the world outside Mullaghduff and jump to her feet, saying, 'Christ, son, we nearly forgot! If we run to the lower rocks, we'll see the fishing boats from Norway going past. Hurry, son, hurry! They're a grand sight on a fine night. Hurry!'

She had no toys or games for me to play with, but she had plenty of ideas for making my stay with her more interesting. We often got up before sunrise to see wild birds flying north through the icy air high above the ocean. Or we sat for hours on the flat rocks below her house watching the big fish attacking smaller ones in the shallow water. Or we went down to the rock pools and caught fish with our bare hands. I know now that these were all simply Granny's ways of entertaining me, but I am also certain that she enjoyed them every bit as much as I did.

Sometimes we used to watch a great passenger ship sail past, its lights shining like stars. Granny would fill the ship with people for me: 'The men handsome and tall, the ladies in rich silks down to their toes, and all of them laughing and dancing and drinking wine and singing. Christ, son, they're a happy old crowd!'

❖

There was a February storm blowing in from the sea the evening the packman fought his way uphill to our door. I watched him through the kitchen window, a tiny shape in the distance, which grew to a man, and then a man with a case as big as himself. When he was a stone's throw from the door, I saw that he was coloured. In those days, packmen were quite common in country areas. They went from house to house with their cases of clothes and bedsheets and cheap jewellery, and if a customer had no money to buy, the packmen were usually willing to take food instead. They had a name for being dishonest.

The sight of this packman put the fear of God into me, because Mother had taught us to keep away from all packmen, and I had never seen a coloured man before in my life. I led Granny to the window and hid behind her.

'Will he attack us?' I whispered fearfully.

'Christ, and if he does, we'll attack him back!' she said bravely and threw open the door. 'Come in, man,' she shouted into the storm. 'Come in and rest, because only a fool like yourself could have made the climb up here today.'

He entered the kitchen backwards, dragging his huge case after him. He dropped into a chair near the door, gasping for breath, too exhausted to speak.

I took a step closer to examine him. He was a young man, no more than twenty, with a smooth brown skin. His head was wrapped in a snow-white turban. His shoulders were narrow, and his feet as small as my younger sister's. Then I saw his hands. They were fine and delicate, and on the third finger of his left hand was a gold ring. It was made to look like a snake, holding a deep red stone between its mouth and its tail. As I watched, the stone seemed to change colour: now it was purple, now rose-pink, now black, now blood-red, now blue. I was still staring at its magic when the packman slid to his knees on the floor and began saying in a low, tuneless voice,

'I sell beau-ti-ful things, good lady, everything for your home. What is it you buy? Silks, sheets, beau-ti-ful pictures for your walls, beau-ti-ful dresses for the lady. What is it you buy?'

As he spoke, he opened his case and removed all that it contained, painting the floor with yellows and greens and whites and blues. It seemed to me he owned all the riches of the world.

'You buy, good lady? What is it you buy?' He spoke without interest, without enthusiasm, too exhausted to care. His eyes never left the ground and his hands spread the splashes of colour around him until he was an island in a lake of brightness.

For a moment, Granny said nothing. There was so much to look at, and it was all so colourful, that she felt quite confused. At the same time she was trying desperately to catch what he was saying, and his accent was difficult for her. When at last words came to her, they broke from her in a sort of cry.

'Ah Christ, sweet Christ, look at them! Look at them! Ah God, how fine they are!' Then rapidly to me, 'What is he saying, son, what? Tell me what it is he's saying.' Then to the packman, 'Ah Christ, mister, they're grand things, mister, grand.'

She knelt down on the floor beside him and gently stroked the surfaces of the clothes. She was silent in amazement, and her mouth opened. Only her eyes showed her delight.

'Try them on, good lady. Try what I have to sell.'

She turned to me to check that she had heard correctly.

'Put on the things you like,' I said. 'Go on.'

She looked at the packman, searching his face to see if he was serious, afraid that he was not.

'I have no money, Mr Packman. No money.'

The packman seemed not to hear. He went on rearranging his colours and did not look up. Only routine kept him going.

'Try them on. They are beau-ti-ful. All.'

She hesitated over the limitless choice.

'Go on,' I said impatiently. 'Hurry up.'

'Everything for the good lady and her home,' said the packman tiredly to the floor. 'Try what I have to sell.'

She made a sudden movement, picking up a red dress and holding it to her chest. She looked down at it, looked to see what we thought of it, and smoothed it out against her, while her other hand pushed her hair back from her face. Then she was absolutely still, waiting for our opinion.

'Beau-ti-ful,' murmured the packman automatically.

'Beautiful,' I said, anxious to have everything tried on and finished with.

'Beautiful,' echoed Granny, softly, slowly. The word seemed new and strange to her.

Then suddenly she was on her feet, dancing wildly around the kitchen. 'Christ!' she screamed. 'You'd make me as much of a fool as you two are. Look at me! See me in a palace, can you?'

Then she went crazy. She threw the dress on the floor, and tried on one thing after another – a green hat and then white gloves and then a blue jacket, all the time singing or dancing or waving her arms, all the time shaking her head, delighted, ashamed, drunk with pleasure.

But soon she grew tired and threw herself, exhausted, on the bed. 'Now, mister, you can take all the damn things away,' she said breathlessly, 'because I have no money to buy anything.'

Again the packman did not hear her, but said tiredly, 'This you like, good lady.' He opened a tiny box, and inside lay six little silver spoons. 'The box to you, good lady, for half price.'

Suddenly Granny was on her feet, dancing wildly round the kitchen.
'See me in a palace, can you?' she screamed.

'Shut your mouth!' she cried, with sudden bitterness, sitting up on the bed. 'Be quiet, Packman! We are poor people here! We have nothing!'

The packman's head bent lower to the ground and he started to gather his things, ready to go out into the darkness.

At once she was sorry for her bad temper. She jumped off the bed and began building up the fire. 'You'll eat with us, Packman, you'll be hungry. We can offer you . . .' She paused and turned to me. 'Christ, son, we'll cook the goose that was to be Sunday's dinner! That's what we'll do!' She turned to the packman. 'Can your stomach hold a good big meal, Packman?'

'Anything, good lady. Anything.'

'A good big meal it'll be, then, and Sunday be damned!'

She took out knives and forks from a drawer. 'Tell me, Packman, what do they call you, what?'

'Singh,' he said.

'What?'

'Singh,' he repeated.

'Christ, but that's a strange name. Sing. Sing,' she said, feeling the sound on her tongue. 'I'll tell you what I'll call you, Packman. I'll call you Mr Sing My Heart's Delight! A good big mouthful. Mr Sing My Heart's Delight!'

'Yes,' he said, quietly accepting her name for him.

'Now, Mr Sing My Heart's Delight, go to sleep for an hour, and when I call you, there'll be a good meal before your eyes. Close your eyes and sleep, you poor exhausted man, you.'

He closed his eyes obediently and in five minutes his head had fallen on his chest.

◈

We ate by the light of an oil lamp. It must have been a month since the packman had last eaten, because he ate fast, like a wild animal, and did not lift his eyes until his plate was cleared. Then he sat back in his seat and smiled at us for the first time.

'Thank you, good lady,' he said. 'A beau-ti-ful meal.'

'You're welcome,' she said. 'Where do you come from, Mr Sing My Heart's Delight?'

'The Punjab,' he said.

'And where might that be?'

'India, good lady.'

'India,' she repeated. 'Tell me, is India a hot country, is it?'

'Very warm. Very warm and very poor.'

'Very poor,' she said quietly, adding the detail to the picture she was making in her mind. 'And oranges and bananas grow there on trees, and the fruit and flowers have all the colours of the rainbow in them?'

'Yes,' he said simply, remembering his own picture. 'It is very beau-ti-ful, good lady. Very beau-ti-ful.'

'And the women,' Granny went on, 'do they wear long silk dresses to the ground? And the men, are the men dressed in purple trousers, and black shoes with silver buckles?'

He spread his hands in front of him and smiled.

'And the women walk under the orange-trees with the sunlight in their hair, and the men raise their hats to them as they pass . . . in the sun . . . in the Punjab . . . in the Garden of Eden . . .'

She was away from us as she spoke, leaving us in the bare kitchen, listening to the wind beating on the roof and the ocean crashing below us. The packman's eyes were closed.

'The Garden of Eden,' said Granny again. 'Where the land isn't bare and so rocky that nothing will grow in it. And you have God's sun in that Punjab place and there is singing and the playing of music and the children . . . yes, the children . . .' The first drops of rain came down the chimney and made the fire spit.

'Christ!' she said, jumping to her feet. 'Up you get, you fools, you, and let me wash the dishes.'

The packman woke with a start, and bent to pick up his case.

'And where are you going?' she shouted to him. 'Christ, man, a wild animal wouldn't be out on a night like this! You'll sleep here tonight. There – in front of the fire. Like a cat,' she added, with a shout of laughter. The packman laughed too.

By the time we had washed the dishes, it was bedtime. Granny and I undressed quickly in the shadowy end of the room, and jumped into the big bed which we always shared.

'Blow out the lamp, Mr Sing My Heart's Delight,' said Granny, 'and then place yourself on the floor there. You'll find a bit of carpet near the door if you want to lie on that.'

'Good night, good lady,' he said. 'Very good lady.'

'Good night, Mr Sing My Heart's Delight,' she replied.

He put the old piece of carpet in front of the fire and stretched himself out on it. Outside, the rain beat against the roof, and inside, the three of us were comfortable and warm.

It was a fine morning the next day. The packman looked young and bright, and his case seemed lighter too. He stood outside the door, smiling happily as Granny directed him towards the villages where he would have the best chance of selling his things. Then she wished him goodbye, in the old Irish way.

'God's speed,' she said, 'and may the road rise with you.'

'To pay you I have no money, good lady,' he said, 'and my worthless things I would not offer you, because . . .'

'Go, man, go. There'll be rain before dinnertime.'

The packman still hesitated. He kept smiling like a shy girl.

'Christ, Mr Sing My Heart's Delight, if you don't go soon, you'll be here for dinner and you ate it last night!'

He put his case on the ground and looked at his left hand. Then, taking off the ring with his long, delicate fingers, he held it out to her. 'For you,' he said very politely. 'Please accept from me . . . I am grateful.'

Even as it lay on his hand, the stone changed colour several times. It had been so long since Granny had been offered a present that she did not know how to accept it. She bent her head and whispered, 'No. No. No.'

'But please, good lady. Please,' the packman insisted. 'From a Punjab gentleman to a Donegal lady. A present. Please.'

When she did not come forward to accept it, he moved towards her and took her left hand in his. He chose her third finger and put the ring on it. 'Thank you, good lady,' he said.

Then he lifted his case, and turned towards the main road. The wind was behind him and carried him quickly away.

Neither of us moved until we could no longer see him. I turned to go round to the side of the house; it was time to feed the chickens and milk the cow. But Granny did not move. She stood looking towards the road with her arm and hand still held as the packman had left them.

'Come on, Granny,' I said crossly. 'The cow will think we're dead.'

She looked strangely at me, and then away from me and across the road and up towards the mountains in the distance.

'Come on, Granny,' I said again, pulling at her dress.

As she let me lead her away, I heard her saying to herself, 'I'm thinking the rain will get him this side of Crolly bridge, and then his purple trousers and silver-buckled shoes will be destroyed. Please God, it will be a fine day. Please God it will.'

Irish Revel

EDNA O'BRIEN

Retold by Clare West

The Irish are said to be good at parties, noisy revels with drinking, singing, and dancing late into the night. But Mary, seventeen and living on a lonely farm, has no experience of them, and as she cycles down the mountain road to her first party in the town, she is full of hopes and dreams and expectations . . .

*M*ary hoped that the ancient front tyre on the bicycle would not burst. Twice she had to stop to put more air in it, which was very annoying. For as long as she could remember, she had been putting air in tyres, carrying firewood, cleaning out the cow shed, doing a man's work. Her father and two brothers worked for the forestry company, so she and her mother had to do everything, and there were three children to take care of as well. Theirs was a mountainy farm in Ireland, and life was hard.

But this cold evening in early November she was free. She rode her bicycle along the road, thinking pleasantly about the party. Although she was seventeen, this was her first party. The invitation had come only that morning from Mrs Rodgers, owner of the Commercial Hotel. At first her mother did not wish Mary to go; there was too much to be done, soup to be made, and one of the children had earache and was likely to cry in the night. But Mary begged her mother to let her go.

'What use would it be?' her mother said. To her, all such

excitements were bad for you, because they gave you a taste of something you couldn't have. But finally she agreed.

'You can go as long as you're back in time to milk the cows in the morning, and don't do anything foolish,' she said. Mary was going to stay the night in town with Mrs Rodgers. She had washed and brushed her hair, which fell in long dark waves over her shoulders. She was allowed to wear the black evening dress that an uncle had sent from America years ago. Her mother said a prayer to keep her safe, took her to the top of the farm road, warned her never to touch alcohol, and said goodbye.

Mary felt happy as she rode along slowly, avoiding the holes in the road, which were covered with thin ice. It had been very cold all day. At the bottom of the hill she got off and looked back, out of habit, at her house. It was the only one on the mountain, small and white, with a piece of land at the back which they called the vegetable garden. She looked away. She was now free to think of John Roland. He had appeared two years before, riding a motorbike daringly fast, and stopped to ask the way. He was staying at the Commercial Hotel and had come up to see the lake, which was famous for the way it changed colour at different times of day. When the sun went down, the water was often a strange reddish-purple, like wine.

'Down there,' she said to the stranger, pointing to the lake below. Rocky hills and tiny fields of bare earth dropped steeply towards the water. It was midsummer and very hot; the grass was tall and there were wild flowers, blood-red, close to their feet.

'What an unusual sight,' he said, looking at the lake.

She had no interest in views herself. She just looked up at the high sky and saw that a bird had stopped in the air above them. It was like a pause in her life, the bird above them, perfectly still. Then her mother came out to see who the stranger was. He introduced himself, very politely, as John Roland, an English painter.

She did not remember exactly how it happened, but after a while he walked into their kitchen with them and sat down to tea.

Two long years had passed since that day, but she had never stopped hoping. Perhaps this evening she would see him. The postman had said someone special in the hotel expected her. It seemed to her that her happiness somehow lit up the greyness of the cold sky, the icy fields going blue in the night, the dark windows of the small houses she passed. Suddenly her parents were rich and cheerful, her little sister had no earache, the kitchen fire did not smoke. Sometimes she smiled at the thought of how she would appear to him – taller and more womanly now, in a dress that could be worn anywhere. She forgot about the ancient tyre, jumped on the bicycle and rode on.

The five street lights were on when she entered the small town. There had been a cattle market that day, and drunken farmers with sticks were still trying to find their own cattle in dark corners of the main street.

As she reached the Commercial Hotel, Mary heard loud conversation inside, and men singing in the bar. She didn't want to go in through the front door, in case someone saw her and told her father she'd gone into the public bar. So she went to the back door. It was open, but she knocked before entering.

Two girls rushed to the door. One was Doris O'Beirne. She was famous for being the only Doris in the whole town, and for the fact that one of her eyes was blue and the other dark brown.

'God, I thought it was someone important,' she said when she saw Mary standing there, blushing, pretty, and with a bottle of cream in her hand. Another girl! There were far too many girls in the town. Girls like Mary with matching eyes and long wavy hair.

'Come in, or stay out,' said Eithne Duggan, the second girl, to Mary. It was supposed to be a joke but neither of the town girls liked Mary. They hated shy mountainy people.

Mary came in, carrying the cream, which her mother had sent to Mrs Rodgers as a present. She put it on the table and took off her coat. The girls whispered to each other and giggled when they saw her dress. The kitchen smelt of cattle and fried food.

Mrs Rodgers came in from the bar to speak to her.

'Mary, I'm glad you came, these two girls are no use at all, always giggling. Now the first thing to do is to move the heavy furniture out of the sitting room upstairs, but not the piano. We're going to have dancing and everything.'

Quickly Mary realized she was being given work to do, and she blushed with shock and disappointment. She thought of her good black dress and how her mother wouldn't even let her wear it to church on Sundays. She might tear it or dirty it.

'And then we have to start cooking the goose,' Mrs Rodgers said, and went on to explain that the party was for Mr Brogan, the local Customs Officer, who was leaving his job.

'There's someone here expecting me,' Mary said, trembling with the pleasure of being about to hear his name spoken by someone else. She wondered which room was his, and if he was likely to be in at that moment. Already in her imagination she was knocking on his door, and could hear him inside.

'Expecting you!' Mrs Rodgers said, looking puzzled for a moment. 'Oh, that young man from the factory was asking about you – he said he saw you at a dance once. A strange one, he is.'

'What man?' Mary said, as she felt the happiness leaking out of her heart.

But Mrs Rodgers heard the men in the bar shouting for her to refill their empty glasses, and she hurried out without replying.

Upstairs Doris and Eithne helped Mary move the heavy furniture out of the sitting room. The two town girls shared jokes with each other, giggled at Mary behind her back, and ordered her around like a servant. She dusted the piano and cleaned the floor. She'd come for a party! She wished she were at home – at least with cattle and chickens it was clean dirt.

Then Eithne and Doris told Mary to get the glasses ready, and they went away to drink a secret bottle of beer in the bathroom.

'She's crying like a baby in there,' Eithne told Doris, giggling.

'God, she looks an eejit in that dress,' Doris said.

'It's her mother's,' Eithne said.

'What's she crying about?' wondered Doris.

'She thought some boy would be here. Do you remember that boy who stayed here the summer before last, with a motorbike?'

'The boy with the big nose?' said Doris. 'God, she'd frighten him in that dress. Her hair isn't natural, either.'

'I hate that kind of long black hair,' Eithne said, drinking the last of the beer. They hid the bottle under the bath.

In the room with the piano Mary got the glasses ready. Tears ran down her face, so she did not put on the light. She saw what the party would be like. They would eat the goose, the men would get drunk and the girls would giggle. They would dance and sing and tell ghost stories, and in the morning she would have to get up early and be home in time for milking. She looked out of the small window at the dirty street, remembering how once she had danced with John on the farm road to no music at all, just their hearts beating, and the sound of happiness.

On that first day at tea, her father had suggested that John should stay with them, and he stayed for four days, helping with the farm work and the farm machinery. Mary made his bed in the morning and carried up a bowl of rainwater every evening, so that he could wash. She washed his shirt, and that day his bare back burnt in the sun. She put milk on it. It was his last day with them. After supper he gave each of the older children a ride on the motorbike. She would never forget that ride. She felt warm from head to foot in wonder and delight. The sun went down, and wild flowers shone yellow in the grass. They did not talk as they rode; she had her arms round his stomach, with the delicate and desperate hold of a girl in love. However far they went, they always seemed to be riding into a golden mist. The lake was at its most beautiful. They stopped at the bridge and sat on a low stone wall. She took an insect off his neck and touched the skin where there was a tiny drop of blood. It was then that they danced, to the sound of singing birds and running water. The air was sweet with the smell of the grass in the fields, lying green and ungathered. They danced.

'Sweet Mary,' he said, looking seriously into her brown eyes. 'I cannot love you because I already have a wife and children to love. Anyway, you are too young and too innocent.'

Next day, as he was leaving, he asked if he could send her something in the post. It came eleven days later – a black-and-white drawing of her, very like her, except that the girl in the drawing was uglier.

'That's no good for anything!' said her mother, who had been expecting a gold bracelet or necklace. They hung it on the kitchen wall for a while and then one day it fell down. Someone (probably her mother) used it, with a brush, for collecting dirt from the floor. Mary had wanted to keep it, to put it safely away in a drawer, but she was ashamed to. Her family were hard people, and it was only when someone died that they ever cried or showed much feeling.

'Sweet Mary,' he had said. He never wrote. Two summers passed. She had a feeling that he would come back, and at the same time a terrible fear that he might not.

In the upstairs room of the hotel the men were taking off their jackets and sitting down to eat. The girls had carried the goose up from the kitchen, and it lay in the centre of the table. Mrs Rodgers had closed the public bar, and now she was cutting meat off the goose and putting it onto plates. She kept Mary busy, serving the potatoes and passing the food around. Mr Brogan, as chief guest, was served first, with the best cuts of goose.

Mary was surprised that people in towns seemed so coarse. When one of the men, Hickey, tried to take her hand, she did not smile at all. She wished she were at home. She knew what her family were doing there – the boys learning their lessons, her mother baking bread, her father rolling cigarettes and talking to himself. In another hour they'd say their prayers and go up to bed. The routine of their lives never changed. The fresh bread was always cool by morning.

O'Toole, the young man who worked at the factory, had bright green eyes and hair so blond it was almost white.

'No one's offered me any food yet,' he said. 'A nice way to behave.'

'Oh God, Mary, haven't you given Mr O'Toole anything to eat yet?' Mrs Rodgers said, and she gave Mary a push to hurry her up. Mary gave him a large plateful, and he thanked her, saying they'd dance later. To him she was far prettier than those good-for-nothing town girls – she was tall and thin like himself.

*Mary would never forget that ride. She felt warm from head to foot,
in wonder and delight.*

And he liked a simple-minded girl with long hair. Maybe later on he'd persuade her to go into another room, and they'd have sex. She had lovely eyes when you looked into them, brown and deep.

The fifth woman at the party was Crystal, the local hairdresser, who had bright red hair, and who did not like the undercooked goose. She and Mrs Rodgers were talking together when Brogan unexpectedly began to sing.

'Let the man sing, can't you,' O'Toole said to Doris and Eithne, who were giggling over a private joke.

Mary felt cold in her thin dress. There hadn't been a fire in that room for years, and the air had not warmed up yet.

'Would any of the ladies care to sing?' asked O'Toole, when Brogan finished. 'I'm sure you can sing,' he said to Mary.

'Where she comes from, they can only just talk,' Doris said.

Mary blushed. She said nothing, but she felt angry. Her family ate with a knife and fork, she thought proudly, and had a cloth on the kitchen table, not a plastic one like this, and kept a tin of coffee in the cupboard in case strangers came to the door.

'Christ, boys, we forgot the soup!' Mrs Rodgers said suddenly, and hurried out with Doris to fetch it from the kitchen.

After the soup, O'Toole poured out four glasses of whiskey, making sure that the level in each glass was the same. There were bottles of beer as well. The ladies had gin and orange.

'Orange for me,' said Mary, but when her back was turned, O'Toole put gin in her orange. They all raised their glasses and drank to Brogan's future. Long John Salmon, the fourth man at the party, asked Brogan about his plans, and Brogan began to talk about the things he wanted to do to his house and garden.

'Come on, someone, tell us a joke,' said Hickey after a while. He was bored with gardening talk.

'I'll tell you a joke,' said Long John Salmon.

'Is it a funny joke?' Brogan asked.

'It's about my brother Patrick,' Long John Salmon said.

'Not that old thing again,' said Hickey and O'Toole, together.

'Oh, let him tell it,' said Mrs Rodgers, who had never heard it.

Long John Salmon told a story about his brother, who died, but came back a month later as a ghost, walking through walls and around the yard.

'Ah God, let's have a bit of music,' said Hickey, who had heard that story nine or ten times. It had neither a beginning, a middle, nor an end.

They put a record on, and O'Toole asked Mary to dance. Brogan and Mrs Rodgers were dancing too, and Crystal said that she'd dance if anyone asked her.

Mary felt strange – her head was going round and round, and in her stomach there was a nice feeling that made her want to lie back and stretch her legs. A new feeling that frightened her. O'Toole danced her right out of the room and into the cold passage beyond, where he kissed her clumsily.

Inside the room, Crystal had begun to cry, sitting at the table with her head on her arms. Gin and orange always made her cry. 'Hickey, there is no happiness in life,' she cried bitterly.

'What happiness?' said Hickey, who was full of drink.

Doris and Eithne sat on either side of Long John Salmon, talking sweetly to him. He was a strange man, but he owned a large fruit farm and he was still single. Brogan, breathless from dancing, was now sitting down, with Mrs Rodgers sitting on his knees. The record finished, and Mary ran in from the dark passage, away from O'Toole, who followed her in, laughing.

O'Toole was the first to cause trouble. He became offended when Mrs Rodgers prevented him from telling a rude joke.

'Think of the girls,' Mrs Rodgers said.

'Girls!' O'Toole said nastily. He picked up the bottle of cream and poured it over the few remaining bits of goose.

'Christ, man!' Hickey said, taking the bottle of cream away.

Mrs Rodgers said it was time everyone went to bed, as the party seemed to be over. All the guests were staying the night at the hotel. The four girls were going to share one room.

In the bedroom Mary sighed. Before they could go to bed, they had to move the heavy furniture back to the sitting room. She could hear O'Toole shouting and singing in another room. There had been gin in her orange, she knew now, because she could smell it on her breath. She had broken her promise to her mother; it would bring her bad luck.

'Ah girls, girls,' O'Toole said, pushing their bedroom door open. 'Where's my lovely Mary? Come out here with me, Mary!'

'Go to bed, you're tired,' Mary said. He caught her hand and started trying to drag her out of the room. She let out a cry.

'I'll throw this flowerpot at you if you don't leave the girl alone,' Eithne called out.

'Stupid cows, the lot of you!' said O'Toole, but he dropped Mary's hand and took a step backwards. The girls rushed to shut the door and push a heavy chest against it, to keep him out.

They all got into the one big bed, two at the top and two at the bottom. Mary was glad to have the other girls with her.

'I was at a party. Now I know what parties are like,' she said to herself, as she tried to force herself to sleep. She heard a sound of water running, but it did not seem to be raining outside. At sunrise she woke up. She had to get home in time for milking, so she put on her dress and shoes and went downstairs.

There was a strong smell of beer. Someone, probably O'Toole, had turned on the taps in the bar, and beer had flowed out of the bar and into the kitchen. Mrs Rodgers would kill somebody. Mary picked her way carefully across the room to the door. She left without even making a cup of tea.

She found her bicycle, but the front tyre was flat, so she walked rapidly, pushing the bicycle. The frost lay on the sleeping windows and roofs. It had magically made the dirty streets look white and clean. She did not feel tired, but simply pleased to be outside, as she breathed in the beauty of the morning.

Mrs Rodgers woke at eight and got out of Brogan's warm bed. She smelt disaster instantly, and ran to call the others. The girls were made to get up and help clean the floors. Hickey, who had by then come downstairs, said what a shame it was to waste good drink. O'Toole, the guilty one, had left early.

'And where's the girl in the black dress?' Hickey asked.

'She ran off, before we were up,' Doris said. They all agreed that Mary was useless and should never have been asked.

'And she was the one who encouraged O'Toole, and then disappointed him, so he got angry,' added Doris.

'I suppose she's home by now,' Hickey said.

Mary was half a mile from home, sitting on the grass. If only I had a boy, someone to love, something to hold onto, she thought, as she broke some ice with her shoe and watched the crazy pattern it made. The poor birds could get no food as the ground was frozen hard. There was frost all over Ireland, frost on the stony fields, and on all the ugliness of the world.

Walking again, she wondered if and what she would tell her mother and her brothers, and if all parties were as bad. She was at the top of the hill now, and could see her own house, like a little white box at the end of the world, waiting to receive her.

The Third Party

WILLIAM TREVOR

■ □ ■

Retold by Clare West

In law, the third party is a person involved in a situation in addition to the two main people involved. A third party quite often appears in cases of divorce, for example.

However, all threesomes are different. And in some of them it is not always clear which of the three people actually is the third party . . .

The two men met by arrangement in the bar of Buswell's Hotel, at half past eleven. 'I think we'll recognize each other all right,' the older man had said. 'I expect she's told you what I look like.'

He was tall, his face pinkish-brown from the sun, his fair hair turning grey. The man he met was thinner, wearing glasses and a black winter coat – a smaller man, whose name was Lairdman.

'Well, we're neither of us late,' Boland said a little nervously. 'Fergus Boland. How are you?' They shook hands. Boland took out his wallet. 'I'll have a whiskey myself. What'll I get you?'

'Oh, just a lemonade for me, Fergus, this time of day.'

Boland ordered the drinks and they stood by the bar. Boland held out a packet of cigarettes. 'Do you smoke?'

Lairdman shook his head. He placed an elbow tidily on the bar. 'Sorry about this,' he said.

They were alone except for the barman, who put their two

glasses in front of them. Boland paid him. 'I mean I'm really sorry,' Lairdman went on, 'doing this to anyone.'

'Good luck,' Boland said, raising his glass. He had softened the colour of the whiskey by adding twice as much water. 'You never drink this early in the day, I suppose?' he said, carefully polite. 'Well, that's very sensible, I always think.'

'I thought it might not be an occasion for drinking.'

'I couldn't talk to you without a drink inside me, Lairdman.'

'I'm sorry about that.'

'You've stolen my wife from me. It's not an everyday event.'

'I'm sorry—'

'It'd be better if you didn't keep saying that.'

Lairdman made no protest at Boland's sharpness. 'The whole thing's awkward, I must confess. I didn't sleep at all last night.'

'You're from Dublin, she tells me,' Boland said, still politely. 'You're in the wood business. There's money in that, no doubt.'

Lairdman was offended. She'd described her husband as clumsy, but had added he wouldn't hurt a fly. Already, five minutes into the difficult meeting, Lairdman wasn't so sure.

'I don't like Dublin,' Boland continued. 'To be honest, I never have. I'm a small-town man, but of course you'll know that.'

He imagined his wife telling her lover about the narrowness of his experience. She liked to tell people things; she talked a lot.

'I want to thank you,' Lairdman said, 'for taking all this so well. Annabella has told me.'

'I don't see that I have any choice.'

Lairdman's lips were very thin, his mouth a line that smiled without any obvious effort. I wonder why he doesn't have a funny little moustache, like so many Dubliners, thought Boland.

'I thought you might hit me when we met,' Lairdman said. 'But Annabella said you weren't like that at all.'

'No, I'm not.'

'That's what I mean by taking it well.'

'All I want to know is what your plans are.'

'Plans?'

'I'm just asking if you're thinking of marrying her, and what your arrangements are. I mean, have you a place that's suitable for her? I'll have another whiskey,' he said to the barman.

'We were hoping that – if you agree – she would move into my place more or less at once. It's suitable all right – a seven-room flat in Wellington Road. But in time we'll get a house.'

'Thanks,' Boland said to the barman, paying him.

'It was my turn to pay,' Lairdman protested, just a little late. She wouldn't care for meanness, Boland thought, when it began to have an effect on her, which it would, in time.

'But marriage?' Boland said. 'It isn't easy, you know, to marry another man's wife in Ireland.'

'Annabella and I would naturally like to be married one day.'

'That's what I wanted to ask you about. How are you thinking of getting a divorce? She doesn't really know much about it – we talked about it for a long time.'

'Thank you for that. And for suggesting we should meet.'

'You two have given me good reasons for a divorce, Lairdman, but it's no damn use to me. A divorce will take years.'

'It wouldn't take so long if you had an address in England. Then we could get a divorce over there.'

'But I haven't an address in England.'

'It's only a thought, Fergus.'

'So she wasn't exaggerating when she said you wanted to marry her?'

'I don't think I've ever known Annabella exaggerate,' Lairdman replied stiffly.

Then you don't know the most important thing about her, Boland thought – that is, she can't help telling lies, which you and I might politely describe as exaggerating.

'I'm surprised you never got married,' he said. He really was surprised, because in his experience self-confident little men like Lairdman very often had a good-looking woman in their life.

'I've known your wife a long time,' Lairdman said softly, trying not to let his smile show. 'As soon as I first saw Annabella, I knew she was the only woman I'd ever want to marry.'

Boland stared into his whiskey. He had to be careful about what he said. If he became angry for a moment, he was quite likely to ruin everything. The last thing he wanted was for the man to change his mind. He lit a cigarette, again offering the packet to Lairdman, who again shook his head. In a friendly, conversational way Boland said, 'Lairdman's an interesting name.'

'It's not Irish – French maybe, or part of it anyway.'

When she had said her lover's name was Lairdman, Boland had remembered it from his schooldays, and in Buswell's bar he had immediately recognized the face. At school Lairdman had been famous for an unexpected reason: his head had been held down a toilet while his hair was scrubbed with a toilet brush. The boys who had done this were older and bigger than him. Called Roche and Dead Smith, they took pleasure in punishing small boys whose faces and habits they found annoying.

'I think we were at school together,' Boland said.

Lairdman almost gave a jump, and this time it was Boland who tried not to smile. Clearly this had come as a shock to Lairdman.

'I don't remember a Boland,' Lairdman said.

'I'd have been a little older than you. I hated the damn place.'

'Oh, I quite liked it,' Lairdman said.

'You day boys went home in the evenings and at weekends, we boarders had to stay there all the time.'

'I suppose that made a difference.'

'Of course it did.'

For the first time Boland felt annoyed. Not only was her lover mean, he was stupid as well. If he had any common sense at all, he'd realize he'd be mad to buy a house for Annabella, because no one could ever be sure she would do what she had promised.

'I've always thought, actually, it gave an excellent education,' Lairdman was saying.

The awful little Frenchman who couldn't make himself understood. The history teacher who gave the class a history book to read while he wrote letters. The mathematics man who couldn't solve the problems he presented. The head teacher who enjoyed causing as much physical pain as possible.

'Oh, a great place,' Boland agreed. 'A fine school.'

'I'm sorry I don't remember you.'

'I wouldn't expect you to.'

'We'll probably send our children there. If we have boys.'

'Your children?'

'You wouldn't mind? Oh dear, no, why should you? I'm sorry, that was a silly thing to say.'

'I'm having another whiskey,' Boland said. 'How about you?'

'No, I'm OK, thanks.'

This time Lairdman didn't mention, even too late, that he should pay. Boland lit another cigarette. So she hadn't told Lairdman? She had let the poor man imagine that in no time at all the seven-room flat wouldn't be big enough for all the children they were going to have. Boland could almost hear her telling Lairdman that her husband was to blame for their childless marriage. In fact, she'd discovered before they got married that she couldn't have children; in a quarrel long after the wedding she confessed that she'd known and hadn't told him.

'Naturally,' Lairdman continued, 'we'd like to have a family.'

'You would, of course.'

'I'm sorry that side of things didn't go right for you.'

'I was sorry myself.'

'The thing is, Fergus, is it OK about the divorce?'

'Are you saying I should agree to be the guilty party?'

'It is what men in your situation usually do, actually. But if you don't like the idea of it—'

'Don't worry, I'll agree to be the guilty party.'

'You're being great, Fergus.'

His wife used to say, 'I think I'll go up and stay with Phyllis,' saying it more often as time went by. Phyllis was a woman she knew in Dublin. But of course Phyllis had just been a name she'd used, a friend who would tell lies for her if necessary. 'Phone me,' he used to say, and obediently his wife phoned him, telling how Dublin looked and how Phyllis was. No doubt she'd been sitting on the edge of a bed in the seven-room flat in Wellington Road.

'It's really good of you to come all this way,' Lairdman said, sounding eager to end the meeting. 'I'll ring Annabella this afternoon and tell her all about it. You won't mind that, Fergus?'

'Not at all.'

Boland had often interrupted such a telephone conversation. He would come home and find her sitting on the stairs, talking on the phone. As soon as he came through the door, she'd wave a greeting and start to whisper secretively into the phone.

The trouble with Annabella was that sooner or later everything in the world bored her. 'Now I want to hear every single thing that's happened since the moment you left home this morning,' she would soon say to Lairdman. And the poor man would begin a long story about catching the bus and arriving at work and having a cake with his coffee. Later, in a quarrel, she would throw it all back at him. 'Who could possibly want to know about your damn cake?' she'd scream wildly at him, her fingers spread out in the air so that her blood-red nail varnish would dry evenly.

'I'll be able to say,' Lairdman was saying, almost proudly, 'that neither of us got angry. She'll be pleased about that.'

Boland couldn't imagine his wife being pleased, since she hardly ever was. He wondered what it was that she liked about Lairdman. When he'd asked her, she'd said her lover was amusing, that he had what she called a fantastic sense of fun.

'I wonder what became of Roche and Dead Smith,' he said.

He didn't know why he said it, why he couldn't accept that the business between them was over. He should have shaken hands with Lairdman and left it at that, perhaps saying there were no hard feelings. He would never have to see the man again; once in a while he would simply feel sorry for him.

'I don't remember either of them,' said Lairdman, shaking his head. 'I'll say goodbye, Fergus. I'm grateful, I really am.'

'They were the boys who had the bright idea of washing your hair in a toilet bowl.'

Boland had said to himself over and over again that Lairdman was welcome to her. He looked ahead to an easy life, living alone. The house she had filled with her moods and her lies for the last twelve years would be as silent as a peaceful sleep. He would clear out the memories of her, because naturally she wouldn't

'You've stolen my wife from me,' said Boland.
'It's not an everyday event.'

do that herself – the old fashion magazines, the empty medicine bottles, the clothes she had no further use for, the curtains torn to pieces by her cats. He would cook his own meals, and Mrs Couglan would still come to clean every morning. Mrs Couglan wouldn't exactly be sorry to see her go, either.

'I don't know why you keep going on about your schooldays,' Lairdman said.

'Let me get you a real drink before you go. Two big ones,' Boland called to the barman.

'No, really,' Lairdman protested. 'Really now.' He had put on his coat and a pair of black leather gloves.

'Oh, go on, man. We're both in need of it.'

Finger by finger Lairdman took one of the gloves off again, and unwillingly picked up the new glass. They drank.

'I only mentioned the school,' Boland said, 'because that was the other thing that you and I shared.'

'As I said, I think we'd maybe send the children there.'

'You don't remember it?' Boland asked.

'What's that?'

'The toilet thing.'

'Look here, Boland—'

'I've offended you. I didn't mean that at all.'

'Of course you haven't offended me. It's just that I see no reason to keep going on about things like that.'

'We'll talk of something else.'

'Actually, I'm getting late.' The second glove was pulled on again, the coat buttons were checked to see that all was well for the street. The glove was removed again when Lairdman remembered there'd have to be a handshake.

'Thanks for everything,' he said.

For the second time, Boland surprised himself by being unable to let the matter rest. 'You mention your children,' he heard himself saying. 'Would these be your and Annabella's children?'

Lairdman's mouth dropped open and he stared at Boland.

'What other children are there?' he asked, shaking his head in a puzzled way.

'She can't have children, Lairdman.'

'Oh now, look here—'

'That's a medical fact. The unfortunate woman is incapable of being a mother.'

'I think you're drunk. One whiskey after another you've had. Annabella's told me a thing or two about *you*, you know.'

'She hasn't told you about the cats she's going to bring with her. She hasn't told you she can't have children. She hasn't told you she gets so bored that her face turns white with anger. It's best not to be near her then, Lairdman. Take my advice on that.'

'She's told me you can't stay sober.'

'Except for occasions like this, I hardly ever drink. I drink a lot less than Annabella does, I can promise you.'

'You've been unable to give Annabella children. She's sorry for you, she doesn't blame you.'

'Annabella was never sorry for anyone in her life.'

'Now look here, Boland—'

'Look nowhere, man. I've had twelve years of the woman. I'm ready to let you take my place. But there's no need for this talk of divorce, I'm just telling you that. She'll come and live with you in your seven-room flat; she'll live in any house you like to buy, but if you wait for ever you won't find children coming along. All you'll have is two cats that want to bite the legs off you.'

'You're being most unpleasant, Boland.'

'I'm telling you the truth.'

'You seem to have forgotten that Annabella and myself have

talked about all this. She knew there'd be bitterness. Well, I understand that. I've said I'm sorry.'

'You're a mean little wooden man, Lairdman. Your head belongs in a toilet bowl. Were you all wet when they let go of you? I'd love to have seen it, Lairdman.'

'Will you keep your damn voice down? And stop trying to quarrel with me! I won't stand here and listen to this.'

'I think Dead Smith went on to become a—'

'I don't care what he became.'

Suddenly Lairdman was gone. Boland didn't even turn his head. After a moment he lit a fresh cigarette. For half an hour he remained alone, where his wife's lover had left him, thinking about his schooldays and Lairdman.

He had lunch in the dining room of the hotel, ordering soup and fish. He imagined himself, one day in the future, entering the silence of his house. He'd actually been born in it. Opposite O'Connor's garage, it was the last one in the town, yellow-painted and ordinary, but a house he loved.

'Did you say the fish, sir?' the waitress enquired.

'Yes, I did.'

He'd got married in Dublin, as Annabella's family lived there. His friends and neighbours had been delighted when he brought her to live among them. They stopped him in the street and told him how lucky he was. But those same people would be delighted when she left. The terrible bitterness that filled her, because of not being able to have children, eventually turned her beauty into a kind of madness. That's what had happened, nothing else.

Slowly he ate his fish. Nobody would mention it much; they'd know what had happened and they'd say to one another that one day, probably, he'd marry again. He wondered if he would.

He ordered a slice of apple cake with cream, and later coffee came. He was glad it was all over. Now he had accepted the truth; it had been necessary to hear it from someone other than his wife. When first she'd told him, he'd wondered if it was all just another of her lies.

He paid his bill and went out to the car park. It was because there hadn't been enough for her to do, he thought, as he drove out of Dublin through the heavy city traffic. A childless woman in a small town had all the time in the world. She had changed the furniture around, and had chosen the wallpaper that her cats had later damaged. But she hadn't joined any clubs or made any friends. He'd driven her to Dublin as often as he could, before she'd started going there alone to visit Phyllis. For years he'd known she wasn't happy, but until she told him he'd never suspected she had become involved with a man.

Lairdman would have telephoned her by now, perhaps to say, 'Why don't you drive up this afternoon?' Maybe all day she had been packing, knowing the meeting at Buswell's was nothing to worry about. The little white Volkswagen he'd bought her might be on the road to Dublin already. He was on the open road now, looking out for the Volkswagen coming towards him. If she passed him, would she greet him with a touch on the horn? Or would he greet her? He didn't know if he would. Better to wait.

But over the next fifty miles or so there was no sign of his wife's car. And of course, he told himself, there was no reason why there should be. It was only his own idea that she might depart that afternoon, and surely she'd need more than a day to pack all her things. The more he thought about it, the less likely it was that she would be capable of completing the move alone.

He turned the radio on, and heard a song called 'Dancing in

the dark'. It reminded him of the world he supposed his wife and Lairdman belonged to, the excitement of secret love, dancing close together in the darkness. 'Poor Annabella,' he said aloud, while the music still played. Poor girl, to have married a small-town businessman like himself. It was lucky, really, that she had met self-confident little Lairdman. He imagined them in each other's arms, and then their shared smile before they held each other close again. As the dull third party, he had no further part to play.

But as Boland reached the first few houses on this side of his home town, he knew none of that was right. The little white car had not carried her to Lairdman today. It would not do so tomorrow or the next day. It would not do so next month, or after Christmas, or in February, or in spring. It would never do so. It hadn't mattered reminding Lairdman of what he had suffered as a schoolboy; it hadn't mattered telling him she was in the habit of lying, or even calling him mean. That kind of unpleasant talk was more or less expected in the situation they found themselves in, and might simply be the result of a few whiskeys. But something had driven Boland to go further. Little men like Lairdman always wanted children. 'That's a total lie,' she'd have said already on the telephone, and Lairdman would have pretended to believe her. But pretending wasn't going to be enough for either of them.

Boland turned the radio off. He stopped the car outside Donovan's pub and sat there for a moment, before going in. At the bar he greeted men he knew, and stood drinking with them, listening to talk of horses and politicians. They left after a few more drinks, but Boland stayed there for a long time, wondering why he hadn't been able to let Lairdman take her from him.

Delivery

LORCAN BYRNE

Retold by Clare West

In her house outside the town, Mrs Kennedy writes her diary, paints the views from her windows, and finds no comfort in the world.

Every week Charlie Blue delivers a box of groceries to her door, but she never appears. It is now one year since the accident . . .

On Thursdays, after the last delivery of the long day, which was to the mad Kennedy woman, Charlie Blue was allowed to keep the van for the night. He could drive home to his mother, proud behind the wheel of the yellow van, waving to any of the boys from his schooldays he might happen to see in their long gardens, playing with their children or cutting their midsummer grass. The arrangement suited his mother. She would have the dinner ready for him and then, after watching their favourite TV programme *Coronation Street* together, he would drive her into town to Horan's Hotel for her weekly game of cards. Tommy Horan also owned the grocery store and she thought he was a great man, a generous man to let her son have the van so that she could get to her game of cards. Charlie said nothing, but knew Tommy Horan to be a bit of a bollocks, selling his tired vegetables and soft tomatoes and eggs that were no longer fresh. He said nothing because his mother could become as nasty as her twelve-year-old dog, which she allowed to sit on her knees while she fed it with the better bits of meat from her dinner plate.

There was a light shower of rain as Charlie was driving to Mrs Kennedy's. The sun appeared strongly again from behind the clouds, the road shone blackly, and the smells of fresh-cut grass and warm earth rose from the fields and came in through the open window of the van. With one hand Charlie took out a cigarette from a packet and lit it with his Horan's Hotel cigarette lighter. He felt lucky. Lucky to have his driver's licence, lucky to have his mother still alive, lucky to be working for Tommy Horan, even if he was an old bollocks.

August 20

A month already. A day just as lovely as that day, the clouds low over the hills. Light seed balls blowing across the land like a first snow. And I hate this beauty because Bobby cannot see it. I paint it but I hate it. With their sharp wings the birds cut open the sky and I am delighted to see it bleed. From my window I can see the gate and the red wallflowers, staining the stones with their blood. At night, the screams of hunted animals comfort me. I am not the only one in pain. In the morning I cannot bear to dress, and prefer to wear only shadows. I go to each of my fifteen windows and decide which view to paint today. I might eat, if my body lets me, and then I move to my chosen window and start to paint.

Charlie drove carefully around the last bend before the Kennedy house. It was a year to the day, he realized, since poor old Foley lost control of his tractor on this very bend and killed Mrs Kennedy's young son. Bobby was his name, only four or five years of age. He and his mother were planting flowers at the foot of the big stone pillars either side of the gate, when around the corner came Foley, shouting about the brakes. The front of the tractor was already too close to the pillar on the left, throwing up grass and earth into the sky. Mikey Tuohy, who saw the whole thing from his field above the road, told the police in detail what happened. His story earned him free beer in the pub for a long time afterwards. He said the screams of the mother nearly stopped his heart. She picked up the boy's body before Tuohy could get there, and she ran all the way up the long driveway to the big house, screaming the whole time as the boy's head dropped lifelessly against her arm and shoulder. Poor old Foley sat on the grass and put his head in his hands and didn't even recognize Tuohy when he reached him. Tuohy said Foley shouldn't have been allowed on the road, not even on a bike, because the old boy was half blind.

✐

September 3

Horan's got somebody new to deliver the groceries. I recognized him: Charles Cullen. He knocked and stood at the door and stared out for a long time, out beyond the fields. At what, I don't know. He stretched his arms out wide like Christ on the cross, to take the whole world to his heart, perhaps. Then he yawned and knocked again. He lifted his T-shirt and scratched his stomach. With his toe he pushed the box nearer the wall, and left slowly, looking back occasionally at the door. While I was emptying the box afterwards I discovered a box of chocolates I hadn't asked for. I must remember not to pay for that.

Now, at the end of summer, the land is bled dry and colours are slowly returning to brown. The cooler air moves against my skin like long grass. When the night enters the house, I look for Bobby. I want to run a bath and pour warm water over his small, smooth back. I want to turn back his soft sheet and lift him into bed and bring the edge of the sheet to his chin. I want to kiss his eyelids as he sleeps. Instead, the darkness tears at my own.

✐

Once, last autumn, as darkness was falling, Charlie saw an owl standing on the right pillar of Mrs Kennedy's gate. It didn't move as Charlie edged the van past the ruined left pillar and wall, and then past the gate still on its side since the accident. At first he thought it was a shadow. He had stopped by the pillar and quietly rolled down the window, when the top of the fat, dark shape turned towards him. From the centre of two wide circles two eyes stared evenly at him, daring him to move, and then with two or three movements of its surprisingly wide wings it slowly, coldly, flew off low over the field towards the trees. Charlie remembered feeling uncomfortable, judged in some way.

✐

October 9

Charles still brings the groceries. For the same reason, I both hate and love him being at my door each week. He reminds me of a better life. I so clearly remember Charles in my class, tall and clumsy at his desk. I had to let him stand in the end. He was freer that way. And the day I decided he had a gift, it comes back so clearly. (I hate the way I can remember every detail of my life before Bobby and Bobby's death!) He brought his finished painting up to my desk and at first I was disappointed. 'A Beach in Summer' it was called, but everything in Charles's painting was a different shade of blue, not just the sea: blue sand, blue hills, blue boat, and what I thought was a blue sun. I asked Charles why he hadn't used other colours, and he said in that frightened way he had, 'Well, Miss, it's a beach at night-time, you see.' Charlie Blue they called him after that. Maybe he still paints. I hope so.

✐

When the police arrived, Mrs Kennedy wouldn't let them into

the house, Tuohy said. Nor the priest either. In the end the police had to break a window and get in that way. They found her upstairs washing the child in the bath. The bloodstained water went everywhere, over the walls and the mirror, wetting the priest and the doctor as they forced the dead boy out of her arms. Dr Murphy phoned his wife, who came over and stayed in the house. Mrs Kennedy didn't come out of the bathroom until the next morning. She came downstairs still covered in blood and told Mrs Murphy to kindly leave her house. Hasn't been seen outside her house and garden since the child was buried. From the high field Tuohy says he sometimes sees her sitting all day at one of her windows. Or walking naked to the woodpile or throwing bits of food out for her cats. As Charlie drove the van up the driveway, he looked around for her, as he always did. He threw the end of his cigarette out of the window, thinking to himself that he had only two cigarettes left and that the old bollocks wouldn't be paying him until tomorrow evening. He'd better save them. He looked up at the high field behind Mrs Kennedy's and guessed that Tuohy was probably spending a lot more time up there than he needed to.

December 25

I found a Christmas cake I hadn't ordered in the box of groceries yesterday.

Sometimes a man comes to the gate and stands there, staring up at the house. Who is he? I wonder. He was there last week and again today.

I feel Bobby's presence strongly today. I fetched the Christmas tree from the cellar and put it in the front room, with coloured lights and pretty glass balls on it. I write in its red and blue and green light. I have wrapped his favourite toys and placed them under the tree. I close my eyes and he is there, lying on the carpet by the tree, opening his presents, turning his blond head around to smile up at me, not minding a bit that they're the same presents as last year. I drink my wine and eat a piece of Christmas cake. Too rich for you, Bobby, too rich.

Charlie couldn't imagine his former art teacher naked. Every other woman in town had spent time naked in his dreams, even Mrs Simpson in the post office. Mrs Kennedy was older than her but not by a million years, she could only be forty or so, and she had had a good shape back then during his time at school, even if it was hidden by long dresses and colourful baggy jackets. He had liked her. She hadn't laughed at him for being stupid. She had put up a painting he had done of a beach at night-time, right up beside the board where everybody could see it. That was good. It was worth being called Charlie Blue for that.

February 18

This week Charlie hid a couple of oranges in the box. I love him for these small presents, the only kisses I receive.

Today the stranger walked up the driveway to the door. I saw him clearly through the glass, tall, blond-haired, blue-eyed. Serious. He just stood there for a long time, unmoving. One of the cats scratched at the kitchen window and I looked away for a moment. When I looked back, he was gone.

Snow fell again today but a hard sun drove it into the hungry grass.

Charlie felt sorry for the thin grey mother cat. She came up to him as he pulled back the side door of the van. He reached down to scratch her head and she replied by rubbing her whole body against the leg of his jeans. It's not much of a life for you, Charlie said, not like you used to have, anyway.

He was halfway to the front door when he saw last week's box exactly where he had left it. A busy line of black ants led from the box to a hole in the front wall of the house. Confused, he walked up and down for a while, looking at the front door and windows. He put the box he was carrying back into the van, lifted his T-shirt and scratched his stomach. Near the corner of the house he saw a torn egg-box and a pile of clean chicken bones.

✎

April 28

I feel so heavy. As the world outside grows lighter and fills with hope, I become heavier. My paintings are still in winter, almost colourless. I paint from one window now, from Bobby's room, which gives the best view of the gate.

My handsome stranger is making good progress. He began by laying out the stones in rows and writing numbers on them. Sometimes he stood up and looked back up at me, serious as always, his blond hair not quite visible from where I sit. The wall is finished. All that remains are the pillar and the gate.

✎

Charlie smoked a cigarette, then knocked on the door for the first time since he began deliveries to Mrs Kennedy nearly a year before. Just leave the box by the door and she'll bring the groceries in herself, Horan had said. But Charlie couldn't just drop the new box down beside the old one and let the ants run all over it. When he knocked, the door opened. It hadn't been properly shut.

'Mrs Kennedy?' he called into the shadowy hall.

✎

When Charlie knocked, the door opened. It hadn't been properly shut.
'Mrs Kennedy?' he called into the shadowy hall.

May 21

Charlie still leaves his small offerings. Yesterday it was a packet of sweets. I cannot eat them but I feel grateful and that feeds me.

I heard the owl call again last night. Closer this time. In my head I could see his long brown body diving from the sky, the terrified movements of the small animal he caught, the slow beat of his wings as he rose into the night-time trees.

The pillar is almost finished. The gate lies on its side on the grass, ready to be put back in place.

Charlie felt cold. These thick-walled country houses were impossible to heat, from a single wood fire, anyway. His eyes got used to the darkness.

'Mrs Kennedy?' he called again. He went into the front room. There was a painting she had been working on, and others standing against a wall which was papered in a flower pattern. An untidy pile of silver knives and forks on the carpet. He closed the door and moved towards the back of the house, where the kitchen was, he supposed. This door was open. He switched on the light. There was a fridge in the corner, still working. Three bananas blackened in a glass bowl. He could see that rats had been here; they had eaten into the bread and the butter and there were even tooth marks in a piece of pink soap in a dish. Charlie went back out into the hall and stood at the bottom of the stairs. He felt colder than ever.

'Mrs Kennedy?' he called and started up the stairs.

June 20

The days are like children, unwilling to come in from their play, and tonight the sky is a gentle purple, as smooth and as tight as the skin of an aubergine.

I have washed all my brushes for the last time. Each one left its own history of colour on my hands. I emptied the wooden knife-and-fork box and put them into it, along with all my paints. My present to you, Charlie Blue.

Tomorrow I will walk through the gate.

The smell of paint-cleaner hangs in the air.

While Charlie waited for O'Reilly the policeman and Dr Murphy to finish inside, he smoked his last cigarette, leaning against the side of the van, looking out over the trees to the distant, darkening hills. A yellow light came from the open doorway and upstairs window of the house. He had just finished his cigarette when O'Reilly came out and handed him a small wooden box, told him to go on home, that the ambulance could take over an hour to get there from Ballinasloe and that there was no point in waiting. O'Reilly would see him tomorrow. Ambulances never hurry for the already dead.

Charlie drove back into town and parked outside Horan's Hotel. The bollocks could keep his van. Through the hotel window he could see his mother at her card game, the dog at her feet. She must have asked a neighbour to bring her into town. The dog sensed his presence, looked out but did not move.

He reached into the van and took out Mrs Kennedy's box of brushes and paints from the passenger seat. Shutting the door with his shoulder, he put her present under his arm and walked on, out past the last lights of the town and into the blue shadows of the moonlit countryside, feeling nervous but welcomed, like a stranger at home in what was once a foreign land.

My Oedipus Complex

FRANK O'CONNOR

❧

Retold by Clare West

*When you are aged about five or six, you are the
most important person in your world and,
naturally, you expect your parents to understand
this and to follow your wishes in everything.*

*But young Larry has a lot of trouble getting
his parents to behave in the right way . . .*

Father was in the army all through the war – the First
World War, I mean – so up to the age of five, I never saw
much of him, and what I saw did not worry me. Sometimes I
woke and there was a big figure in uniform staring down at me.
Sometimes in the early morning I heard the front door bang
and heavy footsteps marching away down the street. These were
Father's entrances and exits. Like Santa Claus, he came and
went mysteriously.

In fact, I rather liked his visits, although there wasn't much
room between Mother and him when I got into the big bed in
the early morning. He smoked a pipe, which gave him a pleasant
smell, and shaved, an interesting activity I had never seen before.
Each time he left a few more souvenirs behind – buttons and
knives and used bullets – packed carefully away in a box. When
he was away, Mother used to let me play with these things. She
didn't seem to think as highly of them as he did.

The war was the most peaceful time of my life. The window
of my room faced south-east. I always woke at first light, and

felt I was rather like the sun, ready to light up the world and be happy. Life never seemed so simple and clear and full of possibilities as then. I put my feet out from under the blankets – I called them Mrs Left and Mrs Right – and invented situations for them. They discussed what Mother and I should do during the day, what Santa Claus should give me for Christmas, and what steps should be taken to brighten the home. There was that little matter of the baby, for example. Mother and I could never agree about that. Ours was the only house in the road without a new baby, and Mother said we couldn't afford one until Father came back from the war, because they were expensive. That showed how silly she was being. The Geneys up the road had a new baby, and everyone knew they didn't have much money. It was probably a cheap baby, and Mother wanted something really good, but I felt she was being too choosy. The Geneys' baby would have been fine for us.

Having arranged my plans for the day, I got up, went into Mother's room and climbed into the big bed. She woke and I began to tell her what I had decided. The bed was so nice and warm that I usually fell asleep beside her, and woke again only when I heard her below in the kitchen, making the breakfast.

After breakfast we went into town, said a prayer for Father at the church, and did the shopping. Mother had all her friends praying for Father, and every night, before going to bed, I asked God to send him back safe from the war to us. It's a pity I didn't know what I was praying for!

One morning I got into the big bed, and there, sure enough, was Father. As usual, he'd arrived like Santa Claus. But later he put on his best blue suit instead of his uniform, and Mother looked very pleased. I saw nothing to be pleased about, because, out of uniform, Father was far less interesting. But she only gave a big smile and explained that our prayers had been answered. We all went off to church to thank God for bringing Father safely home.

Well, I couldn't believe what happened next. When we came back, he sat down and began to talk seriously to Mother, who looked anxious. Naturally, I disliked her looking anxious, because it destroyed her good looks, so I interrupted him.

'Just a moment, Larry!' she said gently.

But when I went on talking, she said impatiently, 'Do be quiet, Larry! Don't you hear me talking to Daddy?'

This was the first time I had heard these awful words, 'talking to Daddy', and I couldn't help feeling that if this was how God answered prayers, he wasn't listening to them very carefully.

'*Why* are you talking to Daddy?' I asked.

'Because Daddy and I have business to discuss. Now don't interrupt again!'

In the afternoon, at Mother's request, Father took me for a walk. I discovered that he and I had quite different ideas of what a walk in town should be. He had no interest in trains, ships, or horses, and the only thing he seemed to enjoy was talking to men as old as himself. When I wanted to stop, he simply went on, dragging me behind him by the hand; when he wanted to stop, I was forced to stop too. I tried pulling him by the coat and trousers, but he was amazingly good at paying no attention to me. Really, it was like going for a walk with a mountain!

At teatime, 'talking to Daddy' began again, made worse by the fact that he now had an evening newspaper. Every few minutes he told Mother some news out of it. I didn't feel this was fair. I was ready to do battle with him any time for Mother's attention, but using other people's ideas gave him an

I tried pulling Father by the coat and trousers, but he was amazingly good at paying no attention to me.

unfair advantage. Several times I tried to talk about something else, but with no success.

'You must be quiet while Daddy's reading, Larry,' Mother said. It was clear that either she really liked talking to Father better than talking to me, or else he had some terrible power over her.

'Mummy,' I said that night in bed, 'do you think, if I prayed hard, God would send Daddy back to the war?'

'No, dear,' she said with a smile. 'I don't think he would.'

'Why wouldn't he, Mummy?'

'Because there isn't a war any longer, dear.'

'But, Mummy, couldn't God make another war?'

'He wouldn't like to, dear. It's not God who makes wars – it's bad people who do it.'

'Oh!' I said, disappointed. I began to think that God wasn't quite as wonderful as people said he was.

Next morning I woke at my usual hour, feeling ready to burst with ideas and plans for the day. I put out my feet and invented a long conversation. Mrs Right talked of the trouble she had with her own father until she put him in the Home. I didn't quite know what the Home was, but it sounded the right place for Father. Then I got up, went into the next room and in the half-darkness climbed into the big bed. Father was taking up more than his fair share of the bed, so I gave him several kicks. Mother woke and put out a hand to me. I lay comfortably in the warmth of the bed with my thumb in my mouth.

'Mummy!' I said loudly and happily.

'Sssh, dear!' she whispered. 'Don't wake Daddy!'

This was a new development, which threatened to be even more serious than 'talking to Daddy'. Life without my early-morning discussions was unthinkable.

'Why?' I asked crossly.

'Because poor Daddy is tired.'

This seemed to me a very poor reason. 'Oh!' I said lightly. 'Do you know where I want to go with you today, Mummy?'

'No, dear,' she sighed.

'I want to go to the river to catch some fish, and then—'

'Don't-wake-Daddy!' she whispered angrily, holding her hand across my mouth.

But it was too late. He was awake. He reached for his matches, lit one and stared in horror at his watch.

'Like a cup of tea, dear?' asked Mother nervously.

'Tea?' he cried angrily. 'Do you know what the time is?'

'And after that I want to go up the Rathcooney Road,' I said loudly, afraid I'd forget something in all these interruptions.

'Go to sleep at once, Larry!' she said sharply.

I began to cry. Father said nothing, but lit his pipe and smoked it, looking out into the shadows away from Mother and me. It was so unfair. Every time I had explained to her the waste of making two beds when we could both sleep in one, she had told me it was healthier like that. And now here was this man, this stranger, sleeping with her without the least care for her health!

He got up early and made tea, but although he brought Mother a cup, he brought none for me.

'Mummy,' I shouted, 'I want a cup of tea, too.'

'You can drink from my saucer, dear,' she said patiently.

That was the end. Either Father or I would have to leave the house. I didn't want to drink from Mother's saucer; I wanted to be considered an equal in my own home. So I drank it all and left none for her. She took that quietly too.

But that night when she was putting me to bed, she said

gently, 'Larry, I want you to promise me that you won't come in and disturb poor Daddy in the morning. Promise?'

That awful 'poor Daddy' again! 'Why?' I asked.

'Because poor Daddy is worried, and doesn't sleep well.'

'Why doesn't he, Mummy?'

'Well, you know that, while he was at the war, Mummy got our money from the post office? Now, you see, there's no more money for us at the post office, so Daddy must go out and find us some. You know what would happen if he couldn't?'

'No,' I said, 'tell me.'

'Well, I think we might have to go out and beg, like the old woman outside the church. We wouldn't like that, would we?'

'No,' I agreed. 'We wouldn't.'

'So you'll promise not to come in and wake him?'

'Promise.'

I really meant it. I knew money was a serious matter and I didn't want to have to beg, like the old woman. So when I woke the next morning, I stayed in my room, playing with my toys for what seemed like hours. I was bored, and so very, very cold. I kept thinking of the big, deep, warm bed in Mother's room.

At last I could bear it no longer. I went into the next room and got into the bed. Mother woke at once with a start.

'Larry,' she whispered, 'what did you promise?'

'But I was quiet for ever so long!' I said miserably.

'Oh dear, and you're so cold!' she said sadly. 'Now if I let you stay, will you promise not to talk?'

'But I want to talk, Mummy,' I cried.

'That has nothing to do with it,' she said, with a firmness that was new to me. 'Daddy wants to sleep. Do you understand?'

I understood only too well. I wanted to talk, he wanted to sleep – whose house was it, anyway?

'Mummy,' I said with equal firmness, 'I think it would be healthier for Daddy to sleep in his own bed.'

That seemed to surprise her, because she was silent for a while. Finally she said, 'Now, you must be perfectly quiet or go back to your own bed. Which is it to be?'

The unfairness of it made me angry. I gave Father a kick, which she didn't notice, but which made him open his eyes.

'Go to sleep again, Mick,' she told him calmly. 'Now, Larry,' she said to me, getting out of bed, 'you must go back.'

This time, in spite of her quiet air, I knew she meant it, and I knew I had to fight back, or lose my position in the home. As she picked me up, I gave a scream loud enough to wake the dead.

'That damn child!' said Father. 'Doesn't he ever sleep?' He turned to the wall, and then looked back over his shoulder at me, with nothing showing except two small, mean, dark eyes.

I broke free from Mother's hold and ran to the furthest corner, screaming wildly. Father sat up in bed.

'Shut your mouth, you young dog!' he said violently.

I was so surprised that I stopped making a noise. Never, never had anyone spoken to me like that before.

'Shut your mouth yourself!' I shouted, mad with anger.

'What's that you said?' shouted Father, jumping out of bed.

'Mick!' cried Mother. 'Don't you see he isn't used to you?'

'I see he's better fed than taught! I'll smack his bottom!'

'Smack your own!' I screamed furiously. 'Smack your own!'

At this he lost his patience and started smacking me. I was so shocked at being hit by someone I considered a complete stranger that I nearly went crazy. I screamed and screamed, and danced in my bare feet. Father, looking clumsy and hairy in nothing but a short army shirt, stared down at me like a mountain ready for murder. It was then that I realized he was jealous, too. And there stood Mother, crying – we seemed to be breaking her heart.

From that morning on, my life was a hell. Father and I were openly enemies. There were many battles between us, he trying to steal my time with Mother, and I trying to steal his. When she was sitting on my bed telling me a story, he pretended he needed her to find a pair of his boots. While he was talking to Mother, I played loudly with my toys. One evening when he came in from work, he found me playing with his souvenirs, and became terribly angry. Mother took the box away from me.

'You mustn't play with Daddy's toys, Larry,' she said firmly. 'Daddy doesn't play with yours.'

Father looked at her, quite shocked. 'Those are not toys,' he said crossly. 'Some of them are very valuable.'

I just couldn't understand why Mother was interested in him. In every possible way he was less likeable than me. He had a workman's accent and made noises while drinking his tea. I thought it might be the newspapers that she liked, so I invented some news of my own to read to her. I tried walking round with his pipe in my mouth, until he caught me. I even made noises while drinking tea, but Mother said I sounded horrible. It seemed to be connected with that unhealthy habit of sleeping together, so I spent a lot of time in their room, but I never saw anything unusual going on. In the end I stopped trying. Perhaps it depended on being grown up and giving people rings. I would just have to wait to find out.

But I didn't want him to think he had won. One day I said, 'Mummy, do you know what I'm going to do when I grow up?'

'No, dear,' she replied. 'What?'

'I'm going to marry you,' I said quietly.

Father gave a great noisy laugh, but I knew he must be

worried. And Mother was pleased. She was probably glad to know that, one day, Father's hold over her would be broken.

'Won't that be nice?' she said with a smile.

'It'll be very nice,' I said confidently. 'Because we're going to have lots and lots of babies.'

'That's right, dear,' she said calmly. 'I think we'll have one soon, and then you'll have someone to play with.'

I was really pleased about that. It showed that in spite of being in Father's power, she still considered my wishes. And anyway, it would show the Geneys that we could have a new baby too.

But the reality was very different. What a disaster it was! Sonny's arrival destroyed the peace of the whole house, and from the first moment I disliked him. He was a difficult child, and demanded far too much attention. Mother was simply silly about him, and thought he was wonderful. As 'someone to play with' he was worse than useless. He slept all day, and I had to be quiet all the time to avoid waking him. It wasn't any longer a question of not waking Father – now it was 'Don't-wake-Sonny!' I couldn't understand why the child wouldn't sleep at the proper time, so whenever Mother's back was turned, I woke him.

One evening, when Father came in from work, I was playing trains in the front garden. I pretended I hadn't noticed him, and said loudly, 'If another damn baby comes into this house, I'm going to leave.'

Father stopped at once and looked at me.

'What's that you said?' he asked sternly.

'I was only talking to myself,' I replied quickly, a little afraid. 'It's private.'

He turned and went inside without a word. I intended it to

be a serious warning, but its effect was quite different. Father started being nice to me. I could understand that, of course. Mother was quite sickening about Sonny. Even at mealtimes she'd get up and look lovingly at him in his little bed, with a foolish smile, and tell Father to look too. He was polite about it, but he looked puzzled – you could see he didn't know what she was talking about. It was painful to see how silly Mother was. Father wasn't good-looking, but he had a fine intelligence. He knew that Sonny was nothing but trouble, and now he realized I knew that, too.

One night I woke with a start. There was someone beside me in my bed. For one wild moment I felt sure it must be Mother – she had understood what was best for her and left Father for ever. But then I heard Sonny screaming in the next room, and Mother saying, 'It's all right, dear, it's all right, Mummy's here.' So I knew it wasn't her. It was Father. He was lying beside me, completely awake, breathing hard and angry as hell.

After a while I realized what he was angry about. What had happened to me had just happened to him. He had pushed me out of the big bed, and now he himself had been pushed out. Mother had no consideration for anyone except that unpleasant child, Sonny. I couldn't help feeling sorry for Father. I had been through it all myself, and even at that age I was prepared to forgive and forget. I began to stroke his back and say, 'It's all right, dear, it's all right.' He didn't seem to like it much.

'Aren't you asleep either?' he said in an angry whisper.

'Ah, come on, put your arm around me, can't you?' I said, and he did, in a sort of way. Cautiously, I suppose, is how you'd describe it. He was very bony, but better than nothing.

At Christmas he made a big effort and bought me a really nice model railway.

Men and Women

CLAIRE KEEGAN

✺

Retold by Clare West

*Children see more than their parents realize.
They may not always understand what they
see, but they have sharp eyes and long ears.
They also know when things aren't right.*

*The daughter of this house is young enough
to believe in Santa Claus at Christmas – but
old enough to want to fight on her mother's
side . . .*

My father takes me with him to places. He has artificial
hips, so he needs me to open gates. To reach our house,
you have to drive up a long narrow road through a wood, open
two lots of gates and close them behind you so the sheep won't
escape to the road. I'm good at that sort of thing. I get out
of the Volkswagen, open the gates, my father drives through,
I close the gates behind him and jump back into the passenger
seat. To save petrol, he lets the car roll downhill, then starts
the engine and we're off to wherever my father is going on that
particular day.

He's always looking for a bargain, so sometimes we go to a
garage for a cheap spare part for the car. Sometimes we end up
in a farmer's dirty field, pulling up young plants we've bought,
to take home and grow on our land. On Saturdays my father
goes to the market and examines sheep for sale, feeling their
bones, looking into their mouths. If he buys a few sheep, he

puts them in the back of the car, and it's my job to keep them there. Da often stops for a meal on the way home. Usually he stops at Bridie Knox's, because Bridie kills her own animals and there's always meat there. The handbrake doesn't work, so when Da parks outside her house, I get out and put a stone behind the back wheel.

I am the girl of a thousand uses.

Bridie lives in a smoky little house, without a husband, but she has sons who drive tractors around the fields. They're small, ugly men whose rubber boots have been mended many times. Bridie wears red lipstick and face powder, but her hands are like a man's.

'Have you a bit of food for the child, missus? There's no food at home,' Da says, making me feel like a starving African child.

'Ah now,' says Bridie, smiling at his old joke. 'That girl looks well-fed to me. Sit down and I'll make some tea.'

'To tell you the truth, missus, I wouldn't say no to a drop of something. I've come from the market, and the price of sheep is shocking, so it is.'

He talks about sheep and cattle and the weather and how this little country of ours is in a terrible state, while Bridie cuts big, thick slices off a large piece of meat. I sit by the window and keep an eye on the sheep in the car. Da eats everything in sight, while I build a little tower of biscuits, lick the chocolate off and give the rest to the sheepdog under the table.

When we get home, I clean out the back of the car where the sheep have been.

'Where did you go?' Mammy asks.

I tell her all about our travels while she and I carry heavy buckets of cattle feed across the yard. Da milks the cow. My brother sits in the sitting room beside the fire and pretends he's studying for his exams next year. My brother is going to be somebody, so he doesn't open gates or clean up dirt or carry buckets. All he does is read and write and do mathematics. He is the intelligent one of the family. He stays in there until he is called to dinner.

'Go and tell Seamus his dinner's on the table,' Da says.

I have to take off my rubber boots before going in.

'Come and have your dinner, you lazy bollocks,' I say.

'I'll tell Da,' he says.

'You won't,' I say, and go to the kitchen, where I put small, sweet garden peas on his plate, because he won't eat boring winter vegetables like the rest of us.

In the evenings, I do my homework on the kitchen table, while Ma watches the television we hire for the winter. On Tuesdays she never misses the programme where a man teaches a woman how to drive a car. Except for a rough woman living behind the hill who drives tractors, no woman we know drives. During the advertising break her eyes leave the screen and travel to the shelf above the fireplace, where she has hidden the spare key to the Volkswagen in an old broken teapot. I am not supposed to know this. I sigh, and continue drawing in the River Shannon on my map.

✱

The night before Christmas, I put up signs. I write THIS WAY SANTA on large pieces of paper. I'm always afraid he will get lost or not bother coming because the gates are too much trouble. I attach the signs to a post at the end of the road, to both gates, and to the door of the sitting room. I put a glass of beer and a piece of cake on the table for him.

Daddy takes his good hat, with a feather in it, out of the cupboard, and puts it on. He looks at himself in the mirror and pulls it on further, to hide his baldness.

'And where are you going?' Mammy asks. 'It's Christmas Eve, a time to stay at home with the family.'

'Going to see a man about a dog,' he says and bangs the door.

I go to bed and have trouble sleeping. I am the only person in my class Santa Claus still visits. But every year I feel there's a greater chance that he won't come, and then I'll be like the others.

I wake early and Mammy is already lighting the fire, smiling. There's a terrible moment when I think maybe Santa didn't come because I said 'you lazy bollocks', but he does come. He leaves me the Tiny Tears doll I asked for, wrapped in the same wrapping paper we have. Santa doesn't come to Seamus any more. I suspect he knows what Seamus is really doing all those evenings in the sitting room, reading magazines and drinking the red lemonade out of the drinks cupboard, not using his intelligence at all.

Only Mammy and I are up. We're the early birds. We make tea, then I help her with the cooking. Sometimes we dance round the kitchen. Seamus comes down to investigate the parcels under the Christmas tree. He gets a dartboard as a present. He and Da throw darts, while Mammy and I put on our coats and feed the cattle and sheep and look for any newly laid eggs.

'Why don't they do anything to help?' I ask her.

'They're men, that's why,' she says simply.

Because it's Christmas morning, I say nothing. I come inside and a dart flies past my head.

'Ha! Ha!' says Seamus.

'Bulls-eye,' says Da.

＊

The day before New Year, it snows. It is the end of another year.

I eat some left-over Christmas food for breakfast and fall asleep watching a film on the television. I get bored playing with my Tiny Tears doll, so I start playing darts with Seamus. When I get a good score, he calls it lucky.

I've had enough of being a child. I wish I was big. I wish I could sit beside the fire and wait to be called to dinner. I wish I could sit behind the wheel of a car and get someone to open the gates for me. Vroom! Vroom! I'd drive away fast.

That night, we get ready for the village dance. Mammy puts on a dark-red dress. She asks me to fasten her pearl necklace for her. She's tall and thin, but the skin on her hands is hard. I wonder if some day she'll look like Bridie Knox, part man, part woman.

Da doesn't make any effort. I have never known him take a bath or wash his hair. He just changes his hat and shoes. Seamus wears a pair of tight black trousers and boots with big heels to make him taller.

'You'll fall over in your high heels,' I say.

We get into the Volkswagen, Seamus and me in the back. Although I washed the inside of the car, I can still smell sheep-dirt. I hate this smell that drags us back to where we come from. Because there are no doors in the back of the car, it's Mammy who gets out to open the gates. I think she's beautiful, with her pearls around her neck and her red skirt flying out as she turns around. I wish Da would get out. I wish the snow would fall on him, not on Mammy in her good clothes. I've seen other fathers holding their wives' coats, holding doors open for them. But Da's not like that.

The village hall stands in the middle of a car park. Inside there's a slippy wooden floor, and benches around the walls, and strange lights that make white clothes seem very bright.

I think Mammy is beautiful, with her pearls around her neck and her red skirt flying out as she turns around.

Everyone we know is there, including Bridie with her red lipstick, and Sarah Combs, who only last week gave my father a glass of wine and took him into the sitting room to show him her new furniture.

There's a band playing dance music, and Mammy and I are first on the floor. When the music stops and restarts, she dances with Seamus. My father dances with the women he knows from his trips. I wonder how he can dance like that, and not be able to open gates. Old men in their thirties ask me to dance.

They tell me I'm light on my feet. 'Christ, you're like a feather,' they say.

After a while I get thirsty and Mammy gives me money for a lemonade and some raffle tickets. A slow dance begins, and Da walks across to Sarah Combs, who rises from her bench and takes her jacket off. Her shoulders are bare; she looks half naked to me. Mammy is sitting with her handbag on her knees, watching. There is something sad about Mammy tonight; it's all around her, like when a cow dies and the men come to take it away. Something I don't fully understand is happening; a black cloud seems to hang in the air. I offer her my lemonade, but she just drinks a little and thanks me. I give her half my raffle tickets, but she doesn't care. Da has his arms round Sarah Combs, dancing close and slow. I go to find Seamus, who's smiling at a blonde I don't know.

'Go and dance with Sarah Combs instead of Da,' I say.

'Why would I do that?' he asks.

'And you're supposed to be intelligent,' I say. 'Bollocks.'

I walk across the floor and tap Sarah Combs on the back. She turns, her wide belt shining in the light.

'Excuse me,' I say, like when you ask someone the time.

She just giggles, looking down at me.

'I want to dance with Daddy,' I say.

At the word 'Daddy' her face changes and she loosens her hold on my father. I take over and dance with him. He holds my hand tight, like a punishment. I can see my mother on the bench, reaching into her bag for a handkerchief. Then she goes to the Ladies' toilets. There's a feeling like hatred all around Da. I get the feeling he's helpless, but I don't care. For the first time in my life I have some power. I can take over, rescue, and be rescued.

There's a lot of excitement just before midnight. Everybody's dancing, knees bending, handbags waving. The band-leader counts down the seconds to New Year and then there's kissing all round.

My parents don't kiss. In all my life, back as far as I remember, I have never seen them touch. Once I took a friend upstairs to show her the house.

'This is Mammy's room, and this is Daddy's,' I said.

'Your parents don't sleep in the same bed?' she said in amazement. That was when I suspected our family wasn't normal.

The hall's main lights are switched on, and nothing is the same. People are red-faced and sweaty; everything's back the way it is in everyday life. The band-leader calls for quiet, and says the raffle is about to take place. He holds out the box of tickets to the blonde that Seamus was smiling at.

'Dig deep,' he says. 'First prize is a bottle of whiskey.'

She takes her time, enjoying the attention.

'Come on,' he says. 'Christ, girl, it's not a million pounds we're offering!'

She hands him the ticket.

'It's a – what colour would ye say that is? It's a pink ticket, number seven two five and 3X429H. I'll give ye that again.'

It's not mine, but it's close. I don't want the whiskey anyway; I'd rather have the box of Afternoon Tea biscuits that's the next prize. There's a general searching in pockets and handbags. He calls out the numbers a few times and is just going to get the blonde to pick another ticket, when Mammy rises from her seat. Head held high, she walks in a straight line across the floor. A space opens in the crowd; people step to one side to let her pass. I have never seen her do this. Usually she's too shy, gives me the tickets and I run up and collect the prize.

'Do ye like a drop of whiskey, do ye, missus?' the band-leader asks, reading her ticket. 'Sure, it'd keep you warm on a night like tonight. No woman needs a man, if she has a drop of whiskey. Isn't that right? Seven two five, that's the one.'

My mother is standing there in her beautiful clothes and it's all wrong. She doesn't belong up there.

'Let's see,' he says. 'Sorry, missus, the rest of the number's wrong. The husband may keep you warm again tonight.'

My mother turns and walks proudly back, with everybody knowing she thought she'd won. And suddenly she is no longer walking, but running, running in the bright white light towards the door, her hair flowing out like a horse's tail behind her.

✳

Out in the car park it's been snowing, but the ground is wet and shiny in the headlights of the cars that are leaving. Moonlight shines down on the earth. Ma, Seamus, and I sit in the car, shaking with cold, waiting for Da. We can't turn on the engine to heat the car because Da has the keys. My feet are as cold as stones. A cloud of steam rises from the window of the chip van. All around us people are leaving, waving, calling out 'Goodnight!' and 'Happy New Year!' They're buying their chips and driving off.

The chip van has closed down and the car park is empty when Da comes out. He gets into the driver's seat, starts the engine and we're off.

'That wasn't a bad band,' he says.

Mammy says nothing.

'I said, there was a bit of life in that band.' Louder this time.

Still Mammy says nothing.

Da begins to sing 'Far Away in Australia'. He always sings when he's angry. The lights of the village are behind us now. These roads are dark. Da stops singing before the end of the song.

'Did you see any nice girls in the hall, Seamus?'

'Nothing I'd be mad about.'

'That blonde was a nice little thing.'

I think about the market, with all the men looking at the sheep and cattle. I think about Sarah Combs and how she always smells of grassy perfume when we go to her house.

We have driven up the road through the wood. Da stops the car. He is waiting for Mammy to get out and open the gates.

Mammy doesn't move.

'Have you got a pain?' he says to her.

She looks straight ahead.

'Can't you open your door or what?' he asks.

'Open it yourself.'

He reaches over her and opens her door, but she bangs it shut.

'Get out there and open that gate!' he shouts at me.

Something tells me I shouldn't move.

'Seamus!' he shouts. 'Seamus!'

None of us moves.

'Christ!' he says.

I am afraid. Outside, one corner of my THIS WAY SANTA sign has come loose; the sign is hanging from the gate.

Da turns to my mother, his voice filled with hate.

'And you walking up there in your best clothes in front of all the neighbours, thinking you won first prize in the raffle.' He laughs unpleasantly and opens his door. 'Running like a fool out of the hall.'

He gets out and there's anger in his walk. He sings, 'Far Away in Australia!' He is reaching up to open the gate, when the wind blows off his hat. The gate opens. He bends to pick up his hat, but the wind blows it further away. He takes another few steps, but again it is blown just a little too far for him to catch it. I think of Santa Claus using the same wrapping paper as us, and suddenly I understand. There is only one obvious explanation.

My father is getting smaller. The car is rolling, slipping backwards. No handbrake, and I'm not out there, putting the stone in position. And that's when Mammy gets behind the wheel. She moves into my father's seat, the driver's seat, and puts her foot on the brake. We stop going backwards.

And then Mammy starts to drive. There's a funny noise in the engine for a moment, then she gets it right, and we're moving. Mammy is taking us forward, past the Santa sign, past my father, who has stopped singing, through the open gate. She drives us through the snow-covered woods. When I look back, my father is standing there watching our tail-lights. The snow is falling on him, on his bare head, on the hat that he is holding in his hands.

Lord McDonald

EAMONN SWEENEY

Retold by Clare West

*Irish music is well known throughout the world.
From Sydney to Buenos Aires, from London to
New York, you can hear an Irish song, dance to
a reel, and take a drop of Irish whiskey.*
  *It is a sad thing, though, to see an Irishman
far from home who is too fond of his glass . . .*

My name is Michael Coleman and they say I am the finest fiddler that ever lived. They say I put a twist to a tune – I add something to it that no one else can. I have never been sure of where the twist comes from. I play that way because it is the only way I know. I play because I have to. I do not know where it comes from or what it is going towards.

My home is a small room in the South Bronx in New York, where the tall buildings shut out the sky. I don't understand the place at all. Two of my nieces passed through the city last week, on their way to look for work. We tried to talk about home but I could not, nor about here either. I picked up the fiddle and played a couple of tunes, and then there was no distance between me and them or The Bronx or Killavil in Ireland where I was born. That's what I have been able to do all my life.

I could talk to you for ever, and still say less than you'd hear from the first few seconds of a tune called 'Lord McDonald'.

It was a calm, bright summer evening. I got the fiddle back once again – I'd had to pawn it because I needed the money. Times were hard, as they have been for years. I remember the days when we musicians were paid a working man's weekly wage for half a morning in the recording studio.

An Irish cop had hired me to play the fiddle at his daughter's birthday party. He had done well for himself since coming to the USA. Not only did he have money, he was also said to be honest. I spent the week before the party drinking to his honesty. A lot of money had been mentioned.

It was a short walk to his house, in good weather. As I went up the wide grey steps to the front door, there was an uneasy feeling in my stomach, the same anxious feeling I always have before I start to play.

Some nights I sit up and play and then I notice the sun has come up and is shining in the street outside. Then I find my face is wet with tears. 'Lord McDonald' is the tune I play.

I knocked at the cop's door, and a beautiful young woman in a blue dress opened it. She looked at me with a face full of puzzlement. There were holes in the elbows of my jacket. Nothing was said for a while.

'I'm Michael Coleman the fiddler. I'm here to play at the birthday party.'

The girl still said nothing, only looked me up and down for a few more moments. Then she turned and ran back inside.

I still remember the face of that cop. It was the face of a man who'd take terrible offence if you weren't enjoying yourself enough at his father's funeral party. A big man, nearly two metres tall, still the colour of a man who's spent many a long summer working on the farm. In a good suit and expensive shoes. He had more of the American accent than he should have had. I could never manage that trick, although I'm not sure I missed much.

The cop rushed across the hall and tried to catch me by the throat. I stepped to one side and he dropped his hands. His right hand was opening and closing; he couldn't keep it still. There was no sound in the neat and tidy evening street. He was so angry that his tongue hit his teeth as he spoke.

'Well, Mickeen Coleman, the great fiddler. Ye dare to show your face here!'

I didn't know what was annoying the man at all.

'My daughter's birthday was this day last week. I had a hundred and fifty people waiting for ye. Damn it, where were ye?'

It's bad when you start making that sort of mistake. I really needed the money he'd have paid me.

'Well, Coleman, where were ye?'

'I made a mistake. I thought it was today I was supposed to be here.'

He banged his hand on the wall by the door. The man was nearly dancing with temper. There were a pair of young women standing in the hall behind him now. They were laughing at his shouting, and that was making him even angrier.

'I'll tell ye why ye weren't here, Mickeen. It's because ye were falling drunk around the South Bronx somewhere. I got plenty of warnings about ye but I didn't take them, fool that I am. Yourself and your friends are a poor advertisement for us Irish, drinking and fighting and bringing our name down in front of the Americans. Ye think ye're something, but ye're nothing.'

'I never aimed to be an advertisement for anyone, only myself.'

'Ye may all be famous but did any of ye ever do anything

to give us a good name, did ye, did ye?' On about the second 'did ye' he hit me in the chest with his right hand and sent me rolling down the steps. I was on my feet before I reached the bottom one. I was always able to land on my feet.

I didn't say anything to the cop. I never even said goodbye. It was a grand evening. There wasn't enough wind to move grass. I just walked off with the fiddle under my arm. Safe.

It cost people a lot more than their fare for the ship when they came over here. Some of them lost all sense of who they were. The cop wasn't the worst of them. A lot of them wouldn't let you near enough their house to be able to throw you off their steps. They'd be ashamed in case someone caught them listening to old Irish tunes like 'The Sligo Maid' or 'The Kerryman's Daughter'. The same people even tried to destroy their accent, cutting bits off it like a man trying to give a block of wood a new shape.

At one time there was always a place for us. A place for those who made others dance. Maybe people don't want to be reminded about what they came from. Because they're frightened they haven't moved as far away from it as they think they have.

The fiddle was pawned again, and I was in a bar. A quiet bar. Drinking whiskey. I learned to drink at those dances where you'd accidentally break a string on your fiddle if they weren't refilling your glass quickly enough. I used to take my whiskey with friends and laughter then. Now I like to drink alone. The drink only makes me feel okay these days. Still, in bad times okay is good.

The twist. That's what they say I have, what I put into a tune that the others can't. You can't try to put the twist into your playing, it has to be part of it. Some days I think I know what the twist is, but I can never catch it because it is inside me.

It is what I am. The drinking, the way I could never stay in one place, the blackness I see in front of me some days, the dreams I have in the night. All there in my fiddle. Whatever it was that was wrong with me leaked out through my fingers, and they heard it as the twist.

And sometimes I think I have nothing to do with it at all. When the first records were sold, 78s they were called, I saw men and women dancing and laughing and crying at the same time. At my playing. I am a farmer's son from Killavil. How could it be me that did that? Maybe the fiddle wasn't the instrument at all.

I heard there were men at home who wouldn't eat for a couple of days so they could buy those records. Men who knew me did that! We had to come to America to record this Irish music to be sent back to Ireland for people there to buy, and yet we'll never see Ireland again. Things are wrong in this world, so they are.

I was never too eager for work. That was well known around the place at home. All I wanted to do was walk the countryside and play music. Some men will kill for land, others will die for a woman. I lived for the music of the dance, fast and slow, sad and sweet.

Everything else on the face of this earth was forgotten when I picked up a fiddle. The coldness of the city meant nothing to me when I was playing well. If I could hear the twist, it meant the life I was living was all right for me.

I'd only just got back to Killavil from London when I came to the USA. Big cars and bright lights, a law against drinking, theatres full of girls singing and dancing, and dollars. You

*You'll always look back at the place you came from
and think it was better.*

couldn't feel right in it unless you were born in it. And even then you might not. You'll always look back at the place you came from and think it was better.

At home we started with an innocent life. Walking home from village dances across pale wet fields, looking at birds on the moonlit lake, playing a tune across the water in the early morning with no other sound in the clear cold air.

But it was a false life. False because it wasn't right to let people live a life like that if they weren't going to be allowed to stay in it, if they were already marked to go someplace else. It didn't prepare us for New York or London, Boston or Manchester.

There was bitterness and jealousy and hunger at home – that's true, I can't say it isn't. But is it fair to be punished with a slow death from a bleeding wound? I look at people's faces when they hear the names of tunes from home, 'The Boys of Ballisodare' and 'The Plains of Boyle', and I know they are dying inside.

The night the cop threw me down the steps, I called at Seamus Anderson's house. I was full of whiskey but I knew he had a fiddle in the house. I wanted to sit up and play music all night. I needed to feel that moment in the back of my head when I would know I'd got there. And then it would disappear before I could catch it, and I would have to try and create it again.

Seamus owned a bar. Like the cop, he lived in a good house in a good area. I managed to open the garden gate, although I couldn't see straight. But I could hear a tune in my head that would cure me if I was only allowed to play it. I never played a tune badly in my life. The drink would change everything around in my head but I would still play the same as ever. The twist would always be there.

I knocked on Seamus Anderson's door. There was light inside but there was no answer. There were plenty of voices. A light came on in the hall, so I tried to concentrate and look sober. Seamus was a churchgoing man who was strongly opposed to drink, although that didn't stop him selling it.

I held my breath and tried to force my eyes to look in the one place at the one time. All it did was make my head go round. I fell against the door. A woman's voice shouted,

'Who's that at this hour of the night?'

'Michael Coleman, tell Seamus Michael Coleman is here to play a tune, to play "Lord McDonald", Michael Coleman has landed from Killavil!'

'Wait there,' she said, and walked away back into the house. I knew that if I didn't get into the light something awful was going to happen. There was a lot of noise inside. It seemed a long while before she came back.

'Seamus Anderson isn't home tonight, he's out of town.'

He had been out of town the last five times I'd been to the house. Still, he was a busy man. A businessman. I still felt bad, so I leaned against the door and hoped the black waves in front of my eyes would disappear. I could hear a man's voice inside the house.

'Is Coleman gone? That man is nothing but trouble when he has drink in him.'

The voice could have been Seamus Anderson's but I was not certain. I banged on the door and shouted for them to let me in. There was another voice. A harder one, with an unpleasant laugh.

'Get out of here, go on, get out of here!' And then to someone else, 'Ye only have to lift him and he'll fall.'

In a narrow back street. Me lying on a pile of rubbish. And

a good number of rats. You'll always know rats because they sit up and look you straight in the eye to let you know that's how carefully they're watching you. I thought these were real rats, not the rats I see when I've had a couple of drinks. 'Lord McDonald' was playing in my head.

There was a cop walking towards me. I realized my nose had been bleeding for a while and the front of my jacket was covered in blood. The cop was cautiously tapping his stick against the inside of his left hand, as he walked slowly towards me.

I stood up and stepped out from the wall. Into the light.

'Officer, I was only taking a rest.'

They take drunks down to the police station and beat them unconscious. With sticks. Sometimes they kill them for the fun of it.

'Christ, it's Michael Coleman, Michael Coleman, the great fiddle player. We've got a whole pile of your 78s at home. What are ye doing here?'

'If I knew that, I wouldn't have to drink.'

He smiled and put a hand under my elbow to stop me falling.

'Good luck, Mr Coleman. It's good to meet ye. Ye're a great fiddler when ye're playing.'

And he walked off. A good Irishman. The rats were still there, so they were real rats. Not my rats. The night was lovely and warm and there was nothing to be afraid of.

♛

The drink is like music. How can you explain it to someone who has not fallen in love with it? How it floods your head and pushes the blood three times faster through your body. The wonderful moment of the first one the morning after, when it starts to clear away the fear and anxiety it put there the night before. Drink makes the world a place of certainty. In every way.

I remember the day I played 'Lord McDonald'. I sat in a small recording studio in the South Bronx at midday. Played another tune for a couple of minutes and then it started. I played the whole of 'Lord McDonald' just once and I could feel something running through me. Every second was like an hour and the music was coming from a place so far back in myself that it was tearing me apart. I followed the music, chased the music, with colours going through my mind and Killavil and my dead brother and the man who taught me to play and the end of all this and the twist in myself and green and brown. It was bringing me somewhere and I finally got there.

I walked away out from the studio when I finished, and two men from the record company came out into the street after me. One of them pulled a huge roll of dollars from a deep trouser pocket.

'Here you are, Michael, a couple of hundred dollars for a special performance. No one ever heard anything like that before.'

The sun was shining the way it does in New York in the summer. The rest of the musicians were sitting in the usual bar, talking about work and spending money. They didn't know then they'd never have that sort of money again.

I tried to explain what had happened. My hand was shaking and the beer was spilling onto the floor. Sunshine was coming through the dark glass of the front window. Blue-coloured light with dust flying round in it. I had got there. I looked at my fingers and said there would be so many more tunes that I would play like this.

But it never came again. Not that way. There was just that one day before it all finished for me. 'Lord McDonald' was the tune. My name is Michael Coleman and they say I am the finest fiddler that ever lived.

A Fishy Story

SOMERVILLE & ROSS

✦ ✦ ✦

Retold by Clare West

The West of Ireland, with its rivers full of salmon, is a grand place to go fishing. Sinclair Yeates has been trying to catch salmon for three days, but without success. He starts his journey home, travelling by train, which in the early years of the twentieth century is an experience full of interest and surprises . . .

People say there is no smoke without fire. But that was not true in the station waiting-room where I had to wait for my train. There was certainly plenty of smoke but the fire seemed quite dead.

When I complained to the stationmaster, he said that any chimney in the world would smoke in a south-easterly wind. He was, however, sympathetic, and took me to his own fire in his office, where the steam rose in clouds from my wet boots. We talked of politics and salmon-fishing, and I had to confess that on my three-day trip I had not caught a single fish.

Before the signal for my train was received, I realized for the hundredth time the wonderful individuality of the Irish mind and the importance of the 'personal element' in Ireland. If you ask people for help, they will break rules, ignore official advice, make special arrangements – all just to please you.

I found a seat in a carriage, and the train dragged itself noisily out of the station. A cold spring rain – the time was the middle of a most unseasonal April – poured down as we came into the open. I closed both windows and began to read my wife's letter again. Philippa often says I do not read her letters, and as I was now on my way to join her and my family in England, it seemed sensible to study again her latest letter of instructions.

'Such bad luck that you haven't caught any salmon. If the worst comes to the worst, and you still haven't by the time you join us, couldn't you buy one?'

I hit my knee with my hand. I had forgotten about the damn fish! Philippa would say, 'Sinclair, I was right! You *don't* read my letters, do you!' It's a pity she never learns from these frequent experiences; I don't mind being called a fool, but then I should be allowed to forget things, as fools do. Without doubt, Philippa had written to Alice Hervey, whose house we were staying in for the next week, and told her that Sinclair would be only too delighted to bring her a salmon. And Alice Hervey, who was rich enough to find much enjoyment in saving money, would have already planned the meal down to the last fish bone.

Anxiously thinking about this, I travelled through the rain. About every six miles we stopped at a station. At one, the only event was that the stationmaster presented a newspaper to the guard; at the next, the guard read aloud some interesting facts from it to the driver. The personal element was strong on this line of the Munster and Connaught Railway. Routine, hated by all artistic minds, was disguised by conversation.

According to the timetable, we were supposed to spend ten minutes at Carrig station, but it was fifteen before all the market people on the platform had climbed onto the train. Finally, the window of the carriage next to mine was thrown open, and an angry English voice asked how much longer the train was going to wait. The stationmaster, who was deep in conversation with the guard and a man carrying a long parcel wrapped in newspaper, looked round and said seriously,

'Well now, that's a mystery!'

The man with the parcel turned away and studied an advertisement, his shoulders shaking. The guard put his hand over his mouth.

The voice, even angrier now, demanded the earliest time its owner could get to Belfast.

'Ye'll be asking me next when I take me breakfast,' replied the stationmaster calmly.

The window closed with a bang, and the man on the platform dropped his parcel, which fell to the ground.

'Oh! Me fish!' cried the man, carefully picking up a remarkably handsome salmon that had slipped out of its wrapping.

Suddenly I had a bright idea. I opened my window and called to the stationmaster,

'Excuse me, would your friend sell me that salmon?'

There was a moment's lively discussion, and the stationmaster replied, 'I'm sorry, sir, he's only just bought it, in this little delay we have. But why don't ye run down and get one for yourself? There are six or seven of them down at Coffey's, selling cheap. There'll be time enough. We're waiting for the mail train to pass through in the other direction, and it hasn't been signalled yet.'

I jumped from the carriage and ran out of the station at top speed, followed by a shout from the guard that he wouldn't forget me. Congratulating myself on the influence of the personal element, I hurried through the town. On my way I met a red-faced, heated man carrying another salmon, who informed me there were still three or four fish at Coffey's, and that he was running for the train himself.

'Coffey's is the house with the boots in the window!' he called after me. 'She'll sell at tenpence a pound if ye're stiff with her!'

'Tenpence a pound,' I thought, 'at this time of year! That's good enough.'

I saw the boots in the window, and rushed through a dark doorway. At that moment I heard, horrifyingly near, the whistle of the approaching mail train. The fat woman who appeared from a back room understood the situation at once, and in one rapid movement picked up a large fish from the floor and threw a newspaper round it.

'Weighs eight pounds!' she said. 'Ten shillings!'

I realized she was charging more than tenpence a pound, but this was not the moment for stiffness. I pushed the coins into her fishy hand, took the salmon in my arms, and ran.

Needless to say, it was uphill, and at the steepest point I heard another whistle, and feared that the worst had happened. When I reached the platform, my train was already out of the station, but the personal element was still working for me. Everybody in the station, or so it seemed to me, shouted loudly to the driver. The stationmaster put his fingers in his mouth and sent an unearthly whistle after the departing train. It took effect; the train slowed. I jumped from the platform and followed it along the rails; there were passengers' heads at all the windows, watching me with deep interest. The guard bent down and helped me up onto the train.

'Sorry, sir, the English gentleman going to Belfast wouldn't let me wait any longer,' he said apologetically.

From Carrig station came a delighted cry from the stationmaster: 'Ye *told* him ye wouldn't forget him!'

My very public return to my seat was greeted with great

When I reached the platform, my train was already
out of the station.

sympathy by the seven countrywomen who were now in my carriage. I was hot and out of breath, and the eyes of the seven women were fixed on me with deep and untiring interest. After a while one of them opened the conversation by supposing it was at Coffey's I got the salmon.

I said it was.

There was a silence, during which it was obvious that one question burnt in every heart.

'She's sure to have asked for ten pence!' said one woman.

'It's a beautiful fish!' I said bravely. 'Eight pounds weight. I gave her ten shillings for it.'

This confession produced a wave of shock and sympathy.

'Sure, and Eliza Coffey would rob her own mother!'

'How could an honest gentleman win a battle with her!'

'Eliza Coffey never paid a penny for that fish! Those boys of hers stole a whole lot of them last night.'

At the next station they climbed out. I helped them with their heavy baskets, and in return they told me I was a fine man, and they wished me well on my journey. They also left me with the information that I was soon to present the highly respectable Alice Hervey with a stolen salmon.

The afternoon passed cheerlessly into evening, and my journey did not get any better. Somewhere in the grey half-light I changed trains, and again later on, and at each change the salmon lost some of its newspaper wrapping. I wondered seriously whether to bury it in my suitcase. At the next station we paused for a long time. Nothing at all happened, and the rain beat patiently on the carriage roof. I closed my eyes to avoid the cold stare of the salmon, and fell asleep.

I woke up in total darkness. The train was not moving, and there was complete silence. I could see a lamp at the far end of a platform, so I knew we were at a station. I lit a match and discovered from my watch that it was eleven o'clock, exactly the time I was supposed to board the mail train. I jumped down and ran along the platform. There was no one on the train; there was no one even in the engine, which was making sad little noises to itself in the silence. There was not a human being anywhere. The name of the station was just visible in the darkness. With a lighted match I went along it letter by letter, but it was so long that by the time I got to the end, I had forgotten the beginning. One thing I did realize, though, was that it was not Loughranny, the station where I had planned to catch the mail train.

For a moment I had the feeling that there had been an accident, and that I now existed in another world. Once more I investigated the station – the ticket office, the waiting room – and finally discovered, at some distance, the stationmaster's office. As I came closer, I could see a thin line of light under the door, and a voice was suddenly raised inside.

'Let's see ye beat that. Throw down your King!'

I opened the door with understandable violence, and found the guard, the stationmaster, the driver, and his assistant seated around a table, playing a game of cards.

I was angry, and with good reason, but I accepted what they said in their defence: they thought there was no one left on the train, a few minutes here or there wouldn't matter, they would soon get me to Loughranny, and the mail train was often late.

Hoping they were right about my chances of making the connection, I hurried back to my carriage, with the officials running enthusiastically ahead of me.

'Watch out for the goods train, Tim!' shouted the stationmaster to the driver, as he banged my door shut. 'She might be coming any time now!'

The answer travelled back proudly from the engine.

'Let her come! She'll have us to deal with!'

The train moved forward and gained speed rapidly. We had about fifteen miles to go, and we went as fast as the engine could manage. But it was no good – we arrived too late.

'Well,' said the guard, as I stepped onto the deserted platform of Loughranny station, 'that old mail is the most unpunctual train in Ireland! If ye're a minute late, she's gone, and maybe if ye were early, ye'd be half an hour waiting for her!'

On the whole, the guard did his best. He said he would show me the best hotel in town, although he feared it would be hard to get a bed anywhere because of the *Feis*. A *Feis*, it seems, is a festival of Irish songs and dances, where people compete for prizes. He picked up my case, he even carried the salmon, and as we walked through the empty streets, he explained to me how easily I could catch the morning boat from Rosslare, and how it was, in fact, quite an improvement on my previous plan.

All was dark at the uninviting door of the hotel chosen by the guard. For five whole minutes we rang the bell hard. I suggested trying a different hotel.

'He'll come,' said the guard confidently. 'He'll come. It rings in his room, so it does.'

A boy, half awake, half dressed, opened the door. 'There's not a bed here,' he said, yawning, 'nor anywhere in the town either.'

'I'll sit in the dining room till the time for the early train,' I said.

'To be sure, there's five beds in the dining room,' he replied, 'and there's mostly two people in every bed.' His voice was firm, but he had a hesitating look in his eye.

'What about the billiard room, Mike?' said the guard helpfully.

'We have blankets on the billiard table at this minute, and the man that won first prize for reels asleep on top of it!'

'Well, can't ye put some blankets on the floor under it?' said the guard, putting my case and the salmon in the hall. 'To be sure, there's no better place in the house! Now I must go home, before me wife thinks I'm dead and buried!'

His footsteps went lightly away down the empty street.

'Nothing troubles *him*!' said the boy bitterly.

And I realized that only the personal element stood between me and a sleepless night on a cold, wet station platform.

✦ ✦ ✦

It was in the dark of the early morning that I woke again to life and its troubles. A voice had woken me, the voice of the first prize for reels, descending through a pocket of the billiard table.

'Excuse me, sir, are ye going on the 5 o'clock train to Cork?'

'No,' I said crossly.

'Well, if ye were, ye'd be late,' said the voice.

I received this useful information in annoyed silence, and tried to wrap myself in a disappearing dream.

'I'm going on the 6.30 meself,' continued the voice, 'and it's unknown to me how I'll put on me boots. Ye would not believe how me feet swelled up in me dancing shoes last night. Me feet are delicate like that, ye see.'

I pretended to be asleep, but the dream was gone. And so was any chance of further sleep.

The first prize for reels got down from the billiard table, presenting an extraordinary picture. He was wearing grass-green breeches, a white shirt, and pearl-grey stockings. He undressed, and put on ordinary clothes, including his painful boots. He then removed himself and his things to the hall, where he had a loud conversation with the boy. Meanwhile, I crawled out of my hiding-place to renew my struggle with life.

Fortunately, the boy soon appeared with a cup of tea.

'I've wrapped the salmon up in brown paper for ye, sir,' he said cheerfully. 'It's safe to take across Europe with ye if ye like! I'll just run up to the station now, with the luggage. Would ye mind carrying the fish yourself? It's on the table in the hall.'

My train went at 6.15. The boy had put my case in one of the many empty carriages, and stayed with me, making pleasant conversation, until the train departed.

'I'm sorry ye had a bad night, sir,' he said, 'and I must tell ye, it was only that Jimmy Durkan – he's the first prize for reels, sir – had taken a few drinks. If he'd been sober, I'd have put a gentleman like ye on the billiard table instead of him. He's a baker, ye know, in the town of Limerick. And he's engaged to my sister. Well, any girl would be glad to marry him. He dances with a beautiful straight back, and he makes grand bread!'

Here the train started.

✦ ✦ ✦

It was late that night when, stiff, dirty, with tired eyes blinded by the bright lights, I was taken by the Herveys' well-trained doorman into the Herveys' huge grand hall, and was told by another of the Herveys' beautifully dressed servants that dinner was over. I was just hoping I could go quietly upstairs to avoid meeting anyone, when a voice cried, 'Here he is!'

And Philippa, looking lovely in evening dress, came into the hall, followed by Alice Hervey, and my niece, whose wedding party this was, and by all the usual relations who hate to miss anything that's going on before a wedding.

'Is this a wedding present for me, Uncle Sinclair?' cried the future bride, in the middle of a flood of questions and sympathy.

As she spoke, she eagerly took hold of the brown-paper parcel that was still under my arm.

'I advise you not to open it!' I cried. 'It's a salmon!'

The future bride gave a little scream of distaste, and without a moment's hesitation, threw it at her best friend, a girl standing near her. The best friend gave an answering scream, and jumped to one side. The parcel that I had looked after with a mother's care across two countries and a stormy sea fell with a crash on the stone floor.

Why did it crash?

'A salmon!' cried Philippa, staring at the parcel. There was now a small pool around it, spreading over the floor. 'But that's whiskey! Can't you smell it?'

The servant came respectfully forward. He knelt down, and cautiously picked pieces of a broken glass bottle out of the brown paper. The smell of whiskey became stronger.

'I'm afraid the other things are ruined, sir,' he said seriously, and pulled out of the parcel, one after the other, a very large pair of dancing shoes, two long grey stockings, and a pair of grass-green breeches.

They were greeted with wild enthusiasm, in doubtless much the same way as when they shared the success of Mr Jimmy Durkan at the *Feis*, but Alice Hervey was not amused.

'You know, dear,' she said to Philippa afterwards, 'I don't think it was very clever of dear Sinclair to take the wrong parcel. I *had* wanted that salmon.'

GLOSSARY

ant a very small insect that lives and works in large groups

aubergine a long vegetable with dark purple skin

billiard room a place where people play billiards (using long sticks to hit balls against each other and into pockets at the edge of a long table)

biscuit a flat, thin, dry cake

blush *(v)* to become red in the face

bollocks *(slang)* someone of bad character; also, a rude word meaning 'nonsense!'

bottom the part of the body that you sit on

breeches short trousers fastened just below the knee

buckles pieces of metal used for fastening shoes

Christ *(in these stories)* an informal *(sometimes offensive)* swear word, used to express surprise or anger, or as a general exclamation in a conversation

coloured *(old-fashioned)* from a race that does not have white skin

cop *(informal)* a police officer

cream the thick yellowish-white liquid that rises to the top of milk

damn *(adj) (informal)* used to describe something or someone you do not like; **damn it** an exclamation of annoyance

dartboard a round board with numbers on it, used in the game of darts; the **bulls-eye** is the centre of the dartboard

doll a child's toy that looks like a small person or a baby

drag *(v)* to pull something along with difficulty

eejit *(Irish English)* an idiot, a very stupid person

exaggerate to make something seem larger, better, worse, or more important than it really is

eyelids the pieces of skin that move to cover your eyes

fair   just, honest, right according to the rules

fiddle *(n)*   a stringed musical instrument usually called a violin;
   fiddler a person who plays the fiddle

the Garden of Eden   (in the Bible) the beautiful garden where
   Adam and Eve lived; a place of happiness and innocence

gentleman   a man of good family who always behaves well

gift   a natural ability

giggle *(v)*   to laugh in a silly way

gin   a strong, colourless alcoholic drink

goods train   a train that carries things, not people

goose   a large bird like a duck, but bigger, which is good to eat

grocery store   a shop which sells food and things for the home

guilty party   (in a divorce) the person who takes the blame for
   breaking up a marriage

hips   the bones at the sides of your body, just below your waist

interrupt   to say or do something that makes somebody stop
   what they are saying or doing

lipstick   something that is used to give colour to the lips

mail train   a train that carries letters and parcels

me *(informal)*   my

milk *(v)*   to draw milk from a cow

missus *(informal)*   used when speaking to a woman

mountainy *(Irish English)*   in or from the mountains

nail varnish   a liquid that people paint on their fingernails

naked   not wearing any clothes

Oedipus complex   a boy's feelings of love for his mother and of
   jealousy towards his father

owl   a bird with large eyes that hunts small animals at night

pawn *(v)*   to leave an object with a person who lends money
   because of this (the object is given back if the money is repaid)

pillar   a stone column that supports a wall

pound   a weight equal to 0.454 kilograms

raffle *(n)* the sale of numbered tickets, one of which wins a prize

recording studio a place where music is put on to cassettes, CDs, computers, etc.

reel *(n)* a fast Irish, Scottish, or American dance, for two or four couples

salmon a large fish with silver skin and pink meat that people eat

Santa Claus an old man with a red coat and a long white beard who, children believe, brings presents at Christmas

scrub to clean something by rubbing it hard with a brush and water

shilling a British coin until 1971, worth 5p in today's money

snake an animal with a very long thin body and no legs

sober not drunk, not affected by alcohol

stationmaster an official in charge of a railway station

stockings thin pieces of clothing that fit closely over the legs and feet

turban a long piece of cloth around the head worn, for example, by Sikh and Muslim men

van a road vehicle that is used for transporting things

ye *(old-fashioned or dialect)* you

ACTIVITIES

Before Reading

Before you read the stories, read the introductions at the beginning, then use these activities to help you think about the stories. How much can you guess or predict?

1 *Mr Sing My Heart's Delight* (story introduction page 1). Choose the most likely answers to these questions.

> 1 In the early 1900s, what might 'a travelling salesman from a faraway land' be selling?
> *pots and pans / carpets / fruit and vegetables / clothes / life insurance*
>
> 2 What is the 'kindness he did not expect'?
> *nursing care / a surprising amount of money / a meal and somewhere to sleep / unusual politeness*

2 *Irish Revel* (story introduction page 12). Do you agree (**Y**) or disagree (**N**) with these ideas?

> 1 Seventeen is the best age to be.
> 2 You remember your first adult party for ever.
> 3 If you look forward to something very much, you often become disappointed.

3 *The Third Party* (story introduction page 24). What do you think about these ideas?

> 1 Two's company, three's a crowd.
> 2 A husband and wife should never divorce.

4 *Delivery* (story introduction page 37). How much can you predict?
Answer these questions.

   1 In the story, will Charlie and Mrs Kennedy meet?
   2 Why does Mrs Kennedy 'find no comfort'?
   3 What happened in the accident?

5 *My Oedipus Complex* (story introduction page 47). What do you
think about these questions?

   1 How do Larry's parents probably feel about him?
   2 What kind of lessons will Larry have to learn in life?

6 *Men and Women* (story introduction page 58). Answer these
questions with your own ideas.

   1 What are the reasons why a daughter might want 'to fight on
   her mother's side'?
   2 Is it good for children to be aware of their parents'
   arguments?

7 *Lord McDonald* (story introduction page 69). Do you agree (Y)
or disagree (N) with these ideas?

   1 Musicians and other creative people are often too fond of
   drinking.
   2 People who live away from home are often very sad people.

8 *A Fishy Story* (story introduction page 79). How much can you
predict? Make some guesses.

   1 Will Sinclair manage to get the salmon he wants?
   2 What will happen to him on his journey home?

ACTIVITIES

After Reading

1 Here are the thoughts of eight characters (one from each story). Which stories are they from, who is thinking, and what has just happened? Choose words from this list to complete the thoughts.

accident, baby, children, ferry, field, freedom, gentleman, meal, present, pride, ring, salmon, school, tears, tune, wheel

1 'It's best she tells him I'm out of town tonight. The man'll have drink in him, as usual. I don't want him in here. He could play a fine _____ once, but it's always the same with these fiddlers from the old country. They destroy themselves with the drink. You'd think they'd have some _____, but not a chance of it.'

2 'Thank God I've got away from him at last! I thought he'd never stop going on about that awful business at _____. Was he lying about her not being able to have _____? Surely she . . . Ah, there's a phone box over there. I'll call her now and ask her . . .'

3 'Such a kind lady! I have never met such a kind lady. To cook a beautiful _____ for me, and to let me sleep by the fire in her house – such kindness! The only way I could thank her was to give her my _____. I will always remember last night . . .'

4 'As God's my witness, there she is, naked as the day she was born. A fine-looking woman. Sure, and she won't care about me looking at her. Poor lady. I still feel bad when I remember the _____ and all. I'll do some more grass-cutting in this _____ again tomorrow . . .'

5 'Right, let's see, take the _____ and get into first gear. Oh, what a terrible noise! I forgot to put my foot on the clutch. That's better. Now a touch of accelerator, release the hand brake, and we're off! Oh, it's a wonderful feeling! _____ at last! I wish I could see the expression on his face!'

6 'Well, that was fortunate, and no mistake! I saw the _____ coming, so I did! But it's a fine _____ he's got, and anyone can see that ten shillings is nothing at all to him . . .'

7 'Did I hear that child right? It could have been *me* speaking! It seems we've both had enough of that damn _____. How can a man enjoy a bit of peace and quiet in his own home with all that yelling and crying going on? Young Larry's got a lot of common sense. I wonder what kind of _____ he'd like for Christmas?'

8 'A last wave to the lovely Mary. That long dark hair shining in the sun, and _____ in those beautiful eyes of hers – all for love of me! It's been a sort of dream for the last few days, but what's the use? Just a couple of hours on the road, and I'll be on the _____ home. I'll take good care that Jane never finds out!'

2 **Here are some remarks and thoughts from the stories. What are the meanings behind the words, do you think? Find the extracts in the story text, then answer these questions.**

1 'God's speed,' she said, 'and may the road rise with you.' *Mr Sing My Heart's Delight* (p 10, line 27)
How would you express this Irish saying in everyday language?

2 'Where she comes from, they can only just talk.' *Irish Revel* (p 20, line 15)
Is this a kind thing to say about Mary? What does Doris mean?

3 'The last thing he wanted was for the man to change his mind.' *The Third Party* (p 27, lines 14/15)
Why is this a surprising sentence at this point in the story?

4 'I love him for these small presents, the only kisses I receive.'
   Delivery (p 42, lines 19/20)
   What does this tell us about Charlie, and about Mrs Kennedy?

5 'I couldn't help feeling sorry for Father.' *My Oedipus
   Complex* (p 57, line 22)
   How has Larry's attitude to his parents changed?

6 'Go and dance with Sarah Combs instead of Da.' *Men and
   Women* (p 64, line 25)
   Why does she say this to Seamus? What is she thinking?

7 'I could never manage that trick, although I'm not sure I
   missed much.' *Lord McDonald* (p 71, lines 1/ 2)
   What is 'that trick', and how does Michael feel about learning
   it?

8 'Routine, hated by all artistic minds, was disguised by
   conversation.' *A Fishy Story* (p 80, lines 25/26)
   What is Sinclair suggesting here about the railway staff?

3 **What happens next in the stories? Write one paragraph for each
   of the three stories below, using the ideas in (1) or (2) to help
   you.**

The Third Party
1 Boland and his wife stay together / share interests
2 divorce / marriage to Lairdman / no children / disappointed

Men and Women
1 Da walks out / gets drunk / found dead
2 Mammy and daughter leave farm / find work / live in town

Lord McDonald
1 recording contract / return to Killavil
2 no money left / sleeping outdoors / picked up by cops

4 Which were your most favourite and least favourite characters in
   these stories? Choose one character for each idea in the list below,
   and explain your choices.

   Which character would you like to . . .
   1 give some advice to?   4 invite to a party?
   2 express your anger to?   5 sit next to on a long flight?
   3 give some comfort to?   6 never meet at all?

5 Here is a short poem (a kind of poem called a haiku) about one
   of the stories. Which of the eight stories is it about?

   > *How can she go on?*
   > *Painting helps to stop the pain*
   > *until summer comes.*

   Here is another haiku, about the same story.

   > *A thoughtful teacher*
   > *recognizes a boy's gift,*
   > *and changes his life.*

   A haiku is a Japanese poem, which is always in three lines, and
   the three lines always have 5, 7, and 5 syllables each, like this:

   | How | can | she | go | on? | = 5 syllables
   | Paint | ing | helps | to | stop | the | pain | = 7 syllables
   | un | til | sum | mer | comes. | = 5 syllables

   Now write your own haiku, one for each of the other seven
   stories. Think about what each story is really about. What are the
   important ideas for you? Remember to keep to three lines of 5, 7,
   5 syllables each.

ABOUT THE AUTHORS

BRIAN FRIEL

Brian Friel (1929–) was born in Omagh in Northern Ireland. He was a teacher before he became a full-time writer. He writes short stories and screenplays, and is one of the best-known Irish playwrights; his most successful play was *Dancing at Lughnasa* (1990). He describes himself: 'I am married, have five children, live in the country, smoke too much, fish a bit, read a lot, worry a lot . . .'

EDNA O'BRIEN

Edna O'Brien (1932–) was born in Twamgraney, County Clare, in Ireland. Her first novel, *The Country Girls* (1960), was followed by many other novels, plays, children's books, and screenplays. She says: 'I write by hand. I do not understand how people can even arrive at a flicker of creativity by means of a computer.'

WILLIAM TREVOR

William Trevor (1928–) was born in Mitchelstown, County Cork, in Ireland. His first novel was published in 1958, and since then he has won many awards for his short stories, novels, and plays. *Beyond the Pale* (1981) is perhaps his best-known short story collection. He says: 'The Irish delight in stories, of whatever kind, because their telling and their reception are by now instinctive.'

LORCAN BYRNE

Lorcan Byrne (1956–) was born in Dublin in Ireland and studied at University College Dublin. His short stories have won a number of prizes, and in 2000 and 2005 he was shortlisted for an award for new Irish writing. He lives in Bray, County Wicklow, in Ireland, and works as a secondary school teacher.

FRANK O'CONNOR

Frank O'Connor (1903–1966), was born Michael O'Donovan, in Cork in Ireland, into a poor family. He had a strong relationship with his mother, which he describes in his book *An Only Child* (1961). He is considered one of the world's best short story writers, and wrote many stories, poems, plays, and novellas, as well as being a travel writer, translator, biographer, and critic.

CLAIRE KEEGAN

Claire Keegan (1968–) was born in County Wicklow in Ireland and grew up on a farm. Her first short story collection, *Antarctica*, which the story *Men and Women* comes from, won the 2000 Rooney prize; her second collection is called *Walk the Blue Fields*. She says: 'I find the short story form deeply attractive. There is a strictness about it which I really admire and it takes your breath away if it's good.'

EAMONN SWEENEY

Eamonn Sweeney (1968–) was born in Sligo in Ireland. He has written two novels, *The Photograph* and *Waiting for the Healer*, sports books, and a play. He appears regularly on radio and TV, writes a sports column for a newspaper, and gives workshops on sports writing. In 1995 he won the European Short Story Award. He lives in West Cork, in Ireland, with his partner and three daughters.

EDITH SOMERVILLE AND MARTIN ROSS

Edith Somerville (1858–1949) was born on the Greek island of Corfu. Her cousin Violet Martin (1862–1915) was born at Ross House, County Galway, in Ireland; she took the name of Martin Ross. The two cousins established a joint literary career, and published many short stories and novels together. *The Irish R.M.*, which *A Fishy Story* comes from, inspired a successful TV series.

OXFORD BOOKWORMS LIBRARY

Classics • Crime & Mystery • Factfiles • Fantasy & Horror
Human Interest • Playscripts • Thriller & Adventure
True Stories • World Stories

The OXFORD BOOKWORMS LIBRARY provides enjoyable reading in English, with a wide range of classic and modern fiction, non-fiction, and plays. It includes original and adapted texts in seven carefully graded language stages, which take learners from beginner to advanced level. An overview is given on the next pages.

All Stage 1 titles are available as audio recordings, as well as over eighty other titles from Starter to Stage 6. All Starters and many titles at Stages 1 to 4 are specially recommended for younger learners. Every Bookworm is illustrated, and Starters and Factfiles have full-colour illustrations.

The OXFORD BOOKWORMS LIBRARY also offers extensive support. Each book contains an introduction to the story, notes about the author, a glossary, and activities. Additional resources include tests and worksheets, and answers for these and for the activities in the books. There is advice on running a class library, using audio recordings, and the many ways of using Oxford Bookworms in reading programmes. Resource materials are available on the website <www.oup.com/elt/bookworms>.

The *Oxford Bookworms Collection* is a series for advanced learners. It consists of volumes of short stories by well-known authors, both classic and modern. Texts are not abridged or adapted in any way, but carefully selected to be accessible to the advanced student.

You can find details and a full list of titles in the *Oxford Bookworms Library Catalogue* and *Oxford English Language Teaching Catalogues*, and on the website <www.oup.com/elt/bookworms>.

THE OXFORD BOOKWORMS LIBRARY
GRADING AND SAMPLE EXTRACTS

STARTER • 250 HEADWORDS

present simple – present continuous – imperative –
can/cannot, must – *going to* (future) – simple gerunds …

Her phone is ringing – but where is it?

Sally gets out of bed and looks in her bag. No phone. She looks under the bed. No phone. Then she looks behind the door. There is her phone. Sally picks up her phone and answers it. *Sally's Phone*

STAGE 1 • 400 HEADWORDS

… past simple – coordination with *and, but, or* –
subordination with *before, after, when, because, so* …

I knew him in Persia. He was a famous builder and I worked with him there. For a time I was his friend, but not for long. When he came to Paris, I came after him – I wanted to watch him. He was a very clever, very dangerous man. *The Phantom of the Opera*

STAGE 2 • 700 HEADWORDS

… present perfect – *will* (future) – *(don't) have to, must not, could* –
comparison of adjectives – simple *if* clauses – past continuous –
tag questions – *ask/tell* + infinitive …

While I was writing these words in my diary, I decided what to do. I must try to escape. I shall try to get down the wall outside. The window is high above the ground, but I have to try. I shall take some of the gold with me – if I escape, perhaps it will be helpful later. *Dracula*

STAGE 3 • 1000 HEADWORDS

... should, may – present perfect continuous – *used to* – past perfect
– causative – relative clauses – indirect statements ...

Of course, it was most important that no one should see
Colin, Mary, or Dickon entering the secret garden. So Colin
gave orders to the gardeners that they must all keep away
from that part of the garden in future. *The Secret Garden*

STAGE 4 • 1400 HEADWORDS

*... past perfect continuous – passive (simple forms) –
would* conditional clauses – indirect questions –
relatives with *where/when* – gerunds after prepositions/phrases ...

I was glad. Now Hyde could not show his face to the world
again. If he did, every honest man in London would be proud
to report him to the police. *Dr Jekyll and Mr Hyde*

STAGE 5 • 1800 HEADWORDS

... future continuous – future perfect –
passive (modals, continuous forms) –
would have conditional clauses – modals + perfect infinitive ...

If he had spoken Estella's name, I would have hit him. I was so
angry with him, and so depressed about my future, that I could
not eat the breakfast. Instead I went straight to the old house.
Great Expectations

STAGE 6 • 2500 HEADWORDS

... passive (infinitives, gerunds) – advanced modal meanings –
clauses of concession, condition

When I stepped up to the piano, I was confident. It was as if I
knew that the prodigy side of me really did exist. And when I
started to play, I was so caught up in how lovely I looked that
I didn't worry how I would sound. *The Joy Luck Club*

MORE WORLD STORIES FROM BOOKWORMS

BOOKWORMS · WORLD STORIES · STAGE 1
The Meaning of Gifts: Stories from Turkey
RETOLD BY JENNIFER BASSETT

BOOKWORMS · WORLD STORIES · STAGE 2
Cries from the Heart: Stories from Around the World
RETOLD BY JENNIFER BASSETT
*Stories from Nigeria, New Zealand, Botswana, Jamaica,
Uganda, Malaysia, India, South Africa*

BOOKWORMS · WORLD STORIES · STAGE 2
Changing their Skies: Stories from Africa
RETOLD BY JENNIFER BASSETT
Stories from Malawi, South Africa, Tanzania

BOOKWORMS · WORLD STORIES · STAGE 3
The Long White Cloud: Stories from New Zealand
RETOLD BY CHRISTINE LINDOP

BOOKWORMS · WORLD STORIES · STAGE 3
Dancing with Strangers: Stories from Africa
RETOLD BY CLARE WEST
Stories from South Africa, Tanzania, Uganda

BOOKWORMS · WORLD STORIES · STAGE 4
Doors to a Wider Place: Stories from Australia
RETOLD BY CHRISTINE LINDOP

BOOKWORMS · WORLD STORIES · STAGE 4
Land of my Childhood: Stories from South Asia
RETOLD BY CLARE WEST
Stories from Sri Lanka, India, Pakistan